Changing the Little Things

By J. L. Manning

J. L. Manning thought that this book would help the common person see how the little things matter. He wrote these twelve unfinished stories into one, hoping that the readers could finish one if not all of the characters stories with encounters from their own lives.

Contents

The Idea

This story begins with an author who got an idea for a new book about changing his world. He didn't think his world needed changing in his opinion. This author was trying to find a way that his research on this new book would come to him easily. Now, this author had plenty of wealth and was happily lazing about his condominium, but he didn't just give up on his idea to change the world.

The author went to a blog that had just locals from within the city where he lived. At this blog, there were people who were complaining about their jobs, their friends, their husbands and wives.

This author logged in to this blog with a common name, John2010, and started out by typing:

John2010: Stop complaining! Change your lives. Change the lives of these people that you are complaining about. Make their lives suit yours. Don't change your lives around theirs.

It took a bit, but someone replied with:

Rick1982: John2010, that is easier said than done.

John2010: Not really. It just takes some work, but no, you want it to come easily. Well, wouldn't it be easier if you had some help?

Rick1982: I may need more help than you can give.

Sally1979: John, how could you help me make my boss to see the truth about me?

John2010: The truth is easy. Getting him to see the truth that you choose can be done too.

Sally1979: Really, what's the plan?

John2010: I.M. me with your E-mail address and I'll email you my idea. Now let's start this plan with 10 people. FCFS.

John sat back for a second when Instant Messages started popping up on his screen. With raised eyebrows, John started copying and pasting these e-mail addresses to the Send To… of his new message.

The message that John had prepared earlier to send to these ten e-mail addresses read:

To my new friends,
The Butterfly Effect is real. It's how you use it that makes the difference. My idea has been used over the years, I'm sure. Read this entire e-mail before deciding that this is a great idea.
You should know these people that you want to change.
You should know what their likes and dislikes are.
You need to put yourself in the position of their likes even if you don't like it.

You need to make them think of their likes and see you.

You need to learn what makes them uncomfortable.

Once you learn these things, you need to learn how to use them. This is where this group comes into play. This group will help you see how others see these people that you are trying to change and how most people see you.

Now you need to see how you and your actions have affected these people that you want to change or make see the truth of your choosing.

Once you have seen how you have affected these people's lives, you can change the things they do by changing how you affect their lives.

You will see how you can just change small things in your life to change how these people affect your life.

Don't bring a friend to join these meetings that we are going to have. In fact, don't tell any friends about this group at all. For the group you will need to write two pages of information about this person that you want to affect. Feel free to use false names and locations.

On these two pages we want to hear how you think everyone else sees the person and how you think this person and most people see you. Third, tell us how you see this person that you want to change. Then tell us how you want to change him/her. This may sound hard, but think about it and you'll see that it is EZ.

This is part of the process. Writing this information down is important, so you can see how these things change. These things have changed and will change in the future. You can shape these changes if you affect these people that you want to change in different ways.

Now I would like you all to reply to this e-mail with three days a week that you can spare an hour for these meetings. I would like us all to meet at this blog in a private room once a week, but I would like to be

available three times a week. I should be able to be on-line in the morning between 6 & 10 and at night between 7 & 11.
John

After John sent this message, he was thinking, *Did I tell them enough? Or did I say too much and they will think it's too much work?*

After that thought passed, John noticed that he had sent eleven e-mails out. *Oh well!* John just shook his head and got another cup of coffee.

By the next morning, all eleven of the bloggers had replied with times between 9:00 and 11:00 pm that would be preferred. John replied to them all with three nights at 10:00 when they could meet. John also said that he scheduled three private rooms for those nights. He thought that they could chat about three specific topics, Work Relations, Family Relations, and Friends.

John was happy this seemed to be working out. He just loved helping people. It would just be a plus if John found that these complaining people's lives were worth writing about.

John was imagining how he should start his book.

The First Meeting

John2010 logged on to the blog site that he had opened with a private room and two subrooms, so he would have three rooms. In the last email he sent this group of eleven, he had added the password to log in to these rooms and asked them not to share it. After logging on to the site at the time he set, he logged in to the private room labeled 11butterflys and found that six people were there.

John2010: I think we should start off with you all posting those two pages I asked you to write. As you can see, the two subrooms are labeled Work and Family, so if you want to change someone at work, even if you are friends with them, post these two pages in the work room. Even if you are friends with the family members, you should post these pages in the family room and any friends that aren't family or at work you should post here.

John was sitting there hoping that these people had more substance to their lives and weren't afraid to share it. Then he shrugged. *Well, I do hear that people share too much on-line. Oh well.*

John2010: I just wanted you all to know that these three rooms are safe and that No One will be sharing this information with anyone.

John rolled his eyes. *I hope they all are willing to share, but the moment someone says it's safe is the moment you should start to doubt them. Then again, it is human nature to trust unless you've learned not to. Maybe I should just keep my mouth shut. Wait, they can't hear me, or read my thoughts for that matter.*

After John shook his head at himself, he saw that four more people had logged in and had posted the two pages in the rooms. John quickly told each room that it was safe to share even though he was sure they already knew not to share too much.

John2010: Please read one of the posts from someone else in the room you have posted in. Then write a reply that would show the author how you think the person that they are trying to change sees them if you were that person.

John sat there glaring at his computer screen reading the posts and waiting for all eleven posts. Now, some were shorter than others. John told himself that was okay. He started to read a post in the Family room, because he thought that these would be simple. There were three posts in this room. After he read the first one, his thought was, *Man, this guy's got problems. Luckily they are mostly in his head.*

John2010: Now, Rick, you have to understand that you are putting a lot of stress on yourself. Don't take that the wrong way. The best thing I can tell you to do is talk to her. Now, we aren't going to tell you to spy on her. We are going to tell you how to talk with her to get the information to ease your mind.

Rick1982: Oh, don't tell me it's just in my head!!!

John2010: Don't leave. Read the reply's from the people here, and don't be offended by any of these comments.

Sledge1984: Rick, I like John's first thought. You should get someone to spy on her. No, no, what I mean is that you should talk to her friends or not friends. People who she is in contact with. Get more info on how she lives her life before jumping to conclusions.

John2010: Now, Rick, I know she is your wife, but you really should make sure you know what she does on her free time. From what I've read, you don't, but you need to tell us more of what you are sure is happening and what you assume is happening.

Rick1982: I hear you…

Rick didn't sign out, but he was unresponsive.

John2010: Sledge, you gave plenty of info and I think your stepbrother is a tease.

Sledge1984: But he's family and he shouldn't be talking to my sister like that.

John2010: I see that you both like the Eagles, so that is a way in, but I see that you don't think he's not all that intelligent, which is okay. You can go with him to a game or one of those weekend rallies you said he goes to and find out how he acts with other women.

Sledge1984: I hate those rallies.

John2010: I read that, but you aren't going for the rally. You are going to find out how he acts with other people. From what I've read, you don't wish to socialize with him, so you don't know enough to judge him. Oh, this is one of those things you do to find out how you can change the person you are trying to change to make your life better.

Sledge1984: Okay, I see what you're saying, that my comments about my stepbrother were one-sided so I should see what the other side looks like.

John2010: That's right, couldn't say it better myself. That was why I asked you all to write about how you think other people see this person that you are trying to change.

Amy1979: Rick, I agree with John that you are being paranoid. You should spend more time with your wife if you are worried about who she's spending time with.

John2010: Amy, I just skimmed your post, but now I have to say the same thing I said to Rick, that you need to find out why your husband is spending that time away from you.

Amy1979: Yes, but he keeps to himself.

John2010: Right. Well, the same thing you need to do is talk to people who your husband is around, but not his best friend. Amy, tell Sledge how you think his sister feels when his stepbrother teases her.

John left the family room and went to the work room to see how they were working out. He found that they had started to chat about how they all were annoyed with their coworkers.

John2010: You are supposed to be giving each other a different view of your lives and encounters. To give a different way to act and change how the person that you are trying to change sees you. Now I have to read your posts and I'll get back to you all.

John read or skimmed through each post to get the main problems down. He saw that the four people in this room were getting it. They had started to tell each other how to change so that they could get closer to the person whom they wanted to change. They were starting to let each other know how they would see them if they acted the way they said. The people in this room had even started to say how to act to the person they were trying to change.

John2010: Now, this is what I'm talking about, getting and giving views on how to get this person to see us differently, so that we can change him/her.

Bill4267: I got this idea, but what if we can't get close to the person we are trying to change?

John2010: Who are this person's friends or who do they not have a choice but to interact with? You have to find a person that you can affect in the person's life that you are trying to change. Then you can use this person to affect the person's life that you want to change. If the person at the desk next to you is having a bad day, then how is your day going to turn out?

Sally1974: That's a good one! Now I see it! The butterfly fly's around you.

Timmy1982: Yeah, why didn't I think of that? The people around you affect you. I'm being sarcastic.

John2010: Timmy, we don't need that. In this room we are just trying to help each other, and don't be funny. Other people who aren't in your head just may get hurt.

Timmy1982: That is funny, but I see. I can be boring.

Jill1959: I've been reading these posts and I've been looking at myself and I still don't see how this is easy.

John2010: Jill, you just need to do one thing that can have a big effect on anybody's life. You just need to learn how to shape that one thing that you need to do to change the world, or at least yours.

Jill1959: Okay, so how am I supposed to make everyone see me as I want?

Bill4267: Well, don't act how you want people to see you. That gets annoying. Find something you can do that may make these people that you've worked with see you as you wish.

John2010: That's right, just bring something new. You can show them something that you've kept personal, and that may make them view you in a new way.

Jill1959: But there are reasons why I keep things to myself.

John2010: I mean something you do outside of work, not that you do in private.

Jill1959: I have hobbies to keep myself busy outside of work.

John2010: That's good. Share your hobbies, but don't expect someone who you don't know well enough not to like your hobby. You shouldn't be scared to share your hobbies with them, because they may have the same hobby.

Timmy1982: That's right, I overheard at lunch some people talking about an outing and I had to look twice. I just couldn't see them being into such things, so I asked and joined them.

John2010: Yes, hobbies and interests are great for bonding with people you don't know. I mean, sports is all men talk about because they want to bond.

Timmy1982: That's funny, male bonding; I thought you said not to be funny.

Bill4267: He meant just you, but yes, Jill, if you want to get ahead, then you need to bond with your coworkers more. I see that you feel isolated. The problem you're talking about is growing, but don't let their preconceptions make you doubt yourself.

Timmy1982: That's right, think positive.

John2010: Yes, but this blog is not just to give advice. It is to help each other change their lives for the better. So, Jill, are you thinking of how you can bond with different people, so that the right people see you as you wish?

Jill1959: I guess I could talk with Jen about knitting and see if she likes to knit.

John2010: Didn't you say that she smokes and has tried to quit? Well, knitting is a way to keep her hands and mind busy. That is a good step, but aren't you trying to relate to the other girls also?

Jill1959: I don't know that they would like knitting or collecting small dancers.

John2010: You may be surprised. Bill, about the people you want to affect, have you had any ideas?

Bill4267: Yes, I have thought of two men to try that with. Jill, you can bond with anyone if you find a common rival.

John2010: That's right, Bill, and write a page about the two men and how you are going to try to change them. All of you should write more detailed posts about the people you are trying to change and the people you are using to change them. Have it for next time, and remember, you are doing this for you. I'm going to check on our friends.

John left the room, thinking, *I have to schedule these three rooms so I have time for them all. What have I gotten myself into?*

John2010: I'm sorry it took so long for me to get here, but I've skimmed the posts about the problems you are having. I see that Tarry1978 has explained my idea. I am glad that I don't need to repeat myself, but, Alex1986, this page isn't for antagonizing.

Tarry1978: I thought I should let them know that this page isn't for complaining.

Alex1986: Sorry, Anna, that was just my first reaction after reading your post.

Anna1983: Yes, I reread my post after your comments and I could see why you'd think that. I am trying to get my friends to take me more seriously.

John2010: Anna and everyone at these pages, you can't change anything if you aren't honest here. So, Anna, don't change your post to how you wish it was, but be honest with yourself. And we are just trying to help.

Tarry1978: Right, I am trying to become more of a part of the group, and I see that I'm not, so I'm not going to make you think that I am. I hope you all have ideas of how to get closer to these girls and not look too needy. I have to go now. I'll see you all next week.

John2010: Yes, and I will email you all about meeting at a different time than the other groups.

Mike1991: Yeah, I was wondering when you were going to show up. I read Anna's post again and saw that a few of my sister's friends are just like her, and I can see why she doesn't want to be thought of that way. The first time I read it I was thinking, "She must be a fun girl." After reading it again, I could see what she wants to change and why.

Anna1983: I just want my friends not to dismiss me as the ditsy girl I once was.

Mike1991: And that job you got. I would think you would want your coworkers to show respect.

Anna1983: They do, but I hear talk that just makes me paranoid, so I dismiss it. Anyway, I think there is a strict work demeanor, so they treat me right.

John2010: I wasn't going to focus on changing yourself. I was hoping you would see that changing the way one person sees you would change other people and in turn would change you. If you want to focus on yourself, then try self-hypnosis. It has done wonders for me.

Anna1983: How do you hypnotize yourself?

John2010: You don't! Why do you have posters of celebrities in your bedroom? Because it makes you feel a certain way. So wouldn't a poster of Einstein make you feel smart? Well, the idea is sound, but let's make it simple. Just take a piece of paper and in big letters write what you want and put it somewhere that you will see it a number of times a day. Even if you don't read it, your subconscious will see it and before long you'll have it.

Mike1991: I've heard that somewhere before, but I never actually did it.

Alex1986: I should try that. Get what you want by writing yourself notes. Good one.

John2010: Try it for your memory problems, Alex. I have on my computer's sidebar a note that just says "John, Don't Forget." I figured that when I see that, my memories come back. Well, I don't forget now.

John finished up with them by asking them to be more specific with the pages that they wrote about how their lives were. Then he read the entire posts that he had saved and wrote specific notes and attached them to this e-mail:

Hi, Friends,

That was a good first meeting. I read the posts in their entirety and I attached my views on them all. You will see that there are eleven attachments in plain text format that you can read in any Word app. I would like to meet each group for a separate hour once a week, so that I can give you all of my attention. You all gave good times for mostly every day, so I can make a schedule that you all should like.

I would like to thank the people who helped out with sharing the idea. I liked how we started on discussing how we might change someone to gain the control that we are looking for. Now we all have to look at ourselves with the opened eyes that the blog meetings are helping with. You all should write new posts like the first one but with what you have learned. Don't use the last post but save it to see how you used to see yourself and the people around you. In less than a month, you should see a change, but you will need to keep these first posts to see how you used to be.

The schedule that you all are waiting for is that I will meet with the Friend Relations on Mondays at 10 pm, the Family Relations on Wednesday at 10 pm, and the Work Relations on Friday at 10 pm. If any of you are going out or just can't be there on one of the nights, then e-mail the group your post. The blog is opened 24/7 so you can meet with each other or me at any time, but please don't share the password.
Thanks All,
John

Monday's Meeting

On Monday the members of the friends group were all logged in to the blog. Even a few people from the other rooms were there to give their opinions. John saw that these other people were logged in and thought, *What I told them, well, it doesn't look as if they are posting. I should say something.*

John2010: I do see that some people from the other rooms are here. You may help out the people in this group. This room is just to discuss the friend relations.

Amy1979: I know I just wanted to see how the other rooms were working out and see if I could help.

Tarry1978: Help is always welcome…

As John was reading, he noticed that the four posts were shorter than the first post, but these posts were more to the point. After John had finished reading the posts, he noticed that the group had started to chat. They all were mostly chatting about how to change how their friends viewed them.

Tarry1978: We have to change the way that the leader of our group of friends sees us.

Mike1991: That's me. I'd like to think, but I can see the one person who has the most impact on my group of friends would be, and it's not the leader.

John2010: That's right, it's not always the leader that you need to change. It could be the one who has the most impact on that leader or the entire group. So you may need to take the group dynamic apart to see who you need to change.

Anna1983: Yes, and my friends have subgroups also. Like the order that my friends choose to ask each other out to a show or something.

Mike1991: Right, but that can change weekly.

John2010: That's right, but why do they change? That is what you need to learn, so you can control when and how they change.

Anna1983: That sounds hard to keep track of.

John2010: That is why I asked you to write these posts down, so you can see the big picture.

Amy1979: Yeah, and that should help make your friendships closer.

Tarry1978: That's right, and the closer you are, the easier it is to control them.

John2010: Yes, and what you want to control is how they see you, so that others see you as they see you. Now, I have had a rude wake-up call telling me that it does matter how a stranger sees me. You all should know why that matters, but if you don't, I'll tell you.

Anna1983: I care what a stranger thinks of me, because it's bad karma to think that anyone has bad thoughts about you.

Mike1991: Well, I have enough to worry about, let alone what someone I don't know thinks of me.

John2010: It matters what the strangers you pass daily say about you, because people talk to each other. I know you've heard of it: gossip. Rumors spread fast, and you never want a bad rumor to get out no matter how small it may seem to you, even if it's not true. If you can start a rumor, then you can change the world, or at least yours…

Tarry1978: Like the rumor that you're CCC. "Cool, Calm, and Collected."

Amy1979: Aren't you???

Alex1986: Sorry I'm late, but I was reading these posts and I think I get it now. My post is too short, but I see that I should be looking for the little things in all of my relationships. I should see what I need to change about myself.

John2010: I wasn't going to be that blunt, but yes. It's how you find it. You should want to change by seeing how you affect people.

Anna1983: Yeah, that's right. I want people to see me as a positive, outgoing contributor to the group.

John2010: How I'm saying to go about it is to look at the other people in your lives. You can find out how they see you and how the other people in their life see you. You can change their views to suit your life first.

Alex1986: Go forth, change the people around you so you can change yourself.

John2010: Simply put, but we all have the concept, so let's see how we can help each other with who we want to change.

Tarry1978: Right. Mike, I was thinking that you need to focus your concern on one person. Your post was the longest today, and I am still wondering what is most important. Do you want to please your friend and his girlfriend or do you want your own girlfriend?

Amy1979: Mike, I agree with Tarry and that old girlfriend of yours seemed cool. If you have a strong connection with someone, nothing ells should matter.

John2010: But it does.

Mike1991: Yeah, because these are new friends and they are cool.

John2010: Why?

Mike1991: Well, they are, and my only close friend just moved away, so I found these guys and they have accepted me.

Anna1983: Mike, it sounds like you have a crush on your new friend's girl.

Mike1991: Oh, don't go there. I know the difference between my illusions.

John2010: That's good, but don't let that hold you back. Just put on the brakes with some people. Illusions can be helpful in this venture. How most people see each other is just an illusion until they look deeper.

Amy1979: But, John, you want us to see past the illusions and build our own to control our friends.

Tarry1978: So, Mike, you need to see past these illusions of these new friends' and see them for what they really are. But I'm afraid that you won't like what you find.

Anna1983: I know what Tarry means, but I'm sure that you are getting something out of this friendship. You just need to look at this friendship more and see how you can shape it.

Tarry1978: Right, you want them to see you as a man who can make his own decisions. You need to bring something to this friendship that you are sure about and show them your confidence.

John2010: Yes, but you want to make sure the leader of the group doesn't just shoot you down. You need to find out what interests him, but what he doesn't share too much.

Amy1979: Right, so you can make it your own thing.

John2010: Mike, you know what you need to do is get closer to Jay and listen. Listening is important for this process to work. You need to listen and write a post so that we can hear it and show you what you may have missed.

Mike1991: Yeah, I get it, but they think I'm gay enough.

Tarry1978: Right, but that's just in your head. Don't let that hold you back.

John2010: That may be the hardest thing to get over. Don't pay any attention to how you think anyone sees you. I know you are what they think you are, but don't assume you know how they think. Stay focused. You can change how people see you from one week to the next. They may not see you how you think they see you. That is what this blog is for, to get a third-eye view on you.

Amy1979: A third eye. Like a third person outside of your conversation.

Anna1983: My friends look down on me sometimes too and get the wrong impression of me. Now it's coming to me how to change that.

Tarry1978: Anna, I was reading your post and it sounds like you need more confidence and that note idea that John told us about... I think that would be good for you.

John2010: Yes, that would work with all of you. You may want to make a recording where you are telling yourself to be more confident and list the things you want. The key here is to listen to the recording every night as you are going to sleep so that it gets drilled in, and believe it or not, you just might be more likely to get it.

Alex1986: I've been reading all of these posts and I see how I should find out more about Nicky. I think he has a lot of influence over my friends, but he is usually the quiet one.

Tarry1978: I see that and your girlfriends seem to be there for him, not you as much. I'm sure that your girlfriend gives you a different kind of attention, but get close to him and she may see you with a different light.

John2010: Yes, you all should be on the lookout for little things that may make a big difference on how your friends see you. Write about the thing that you may not see as clear, but affects your friends. Anna, you know that girl you think is annoying? Well, you should find out what your friends like about her and use that.

Anna1983: Yeah, I guess, but we don't get along that well.

Alex1986: I think that John is saying that getting to know your friends new friend better is one of those things that you may not like but you do it to get the upper hand.

Anna1983: I do like her boyfriend, so I guess I could get closer to him by standing her company.

John2010: Wait, you don't want to make it known that all you're into is her boyfriend. You need to find something that you can enjoy with her, not just with her boyfriend.

Amy1979: That's right, you may lose that group of friends if you act like a skank.

Anna1983: I think they know I like Todd, but I'm not a boyfriend chaser.

John2010: You don't want to make your friends not like you, but it is okay if they are upset with you for a week. Okay, I should go. I see that Alex and Tarry have left.

After John rereads all of the posts, he wrote one or two paragraphs to the four members of the Friend Relations Group. John pointed out in detail what he thought they needed to do to get the outcome that they wished for. John thought about sending them each the pages from the blog, but he thought twice. *Now, I'm writing a book, so I'm not going to give these people the chance to compare their posts to my book after I've sold thousands of copies.*

Wednesday's Group

John logged in to the blog and saw that Amy's post had good details but Sledge's not so much. Rick hadn't logged in yet, but Amy noticed how short Sledge's post was and told him all about what John had told the friends group on Monday.

John2010: Thanks, Amy, I hate repeating myself, but, Sledge, I can tell that you are acting friendlier with your in-laws and getting closer to Andy.

Sledge1984: Yeah, and it's hard. I tried to spend Saturday with them, but Andy kept acting out. He wasn't flirting with my sister as much, because there was a game on that I tried to keep interest in. I had trouble with that, but after the game I actually talked with him.

Amy1979: It looks like you will be getting together again this weekend.

John2010: Yes, that is a good start. Now you need to see how to find common ground. You need to pay attention to his interests.

Sledge1984: Well, I don't like racing, but we should be going to a rally next weekend, so I might find something interesting there.

Amy1979: That sounds like fun.

John2010: You should research what it's about and find an interest to bond with Andy on.

Sledge1984: I don't know that I want to bond with him.

John2010: Well, you want to find a way to get to know him, so you need to spend time with him to find how you can control him.

Rick1982: Sledge, it is easier than you think. I was talking with my wife's friends, but not her best friends. Then I approached her about it and we really talked. I wrote a whole page about it.

Sledge1984: I saw your long post pop up.

Rick1982: Sledge, I saw your short post and I get that you don't like how Andy acts out. I'm not sure how he's acting out. I like acting out in celebration with my friends, but I hate it when my cousin acts out and start screaming.

John2010: Yes Sledge, I would like you to write how Andy acts out. I get the feeling that he is being too aggressive for your taste.

Amy1979: It sounds like you just needed to listen to your wife better, Rick.

Rick1982: Right. Well, I do listen, but it's how I approached her that made the difference. It's just so annoying how personal she takes the little things.

John2010: You have to be careful with people like that.

Rick1982: Don't I know it?

John2010: Yes, well, you don't want to feel like you're walking on eggshells, so you need to let her know that it makes you uncomfortable that she is too sensitive about things.

Sledge1984: Rick, it sounds as if she hasn't always been so sensitive, so what has changed?

Rick1982: I think it's something at work, but I'm not sure if it's a man or what.

John2010: Rick, do not jump to conclusions, but my first thought is that she was mistreated in some way to make her change. Now, it may be that a friend was mistreated that she has been there for.

Sledge1984: That's right, my sister acts crazy sometimes, and since we are close I stop her and ask what's wrong and it usually is a friend of hers is having trouble with a boyfriend.

Amy1979: Yeah, I hate to hear that my friends are having trouble, but don't act too interested in her friends. You need to make sure she knows that she is who you are concerned with.

Rick1982: I'm not that close with any of my wife's friends, so I had to call her workplace and talk to a stranger to find out what she's like at work.

John2010: That's okay, but you may want to let her friends know that you are worried. The fact that you told that person you talked to on the phone not to tell her you called made it seem like you're hiding something.

Sledge1984: My wife hates it when she thinks I have a secret.

Rick1982: Right, right, I have to let her know that I'm concerned, but what if she has a secret?

John2010: One thing at a time. You need to find out what has changed in her life, then see how you can use that to change her back. We all change and we'll never be what we once were, but you can bend her the way that you wish her to be.

Sledge1984: Right, you don't want to break her, just bend her.

John2010: Now, Amy, it looks like you're finding that your husband has new friends and you think you should meet them and try to become part of the group.

Amy1979: But I'm not sure, that I like these new friends.

Sledge1984: Right, but are you friends with his other friends?

Amy1979: Yes, I think so.

Rick1982: Well, I think I know what Sledge is getting at. From what you have told us, you are a big part of your husband's life.

Amy1979: Right, I'm his wife.

Sledge1984: Well, putting it simply, you are smothering him. I like attention, but the right kind and not too much.

John2010: Now, Amy, don't take this the wrong way. We aren't judging you, but from what you have told us, you like to be in control. That is okay, that is what we are trying to gain. You just can't let the person know you always are in control.

Amy1979: You guys are talking like I'm a control freak.

Rick1982: I couldn't have said it better. Your husband feels like you have become a control freak. That's why he has new friends.

Sledge1984: Yeah, I hate it when my sister got a new friend that I didn't like, but it just hit me. I was too close with her friends and I guess she wanted friends that I wouldn't be such friends with.

John2010: Amy, your husband is just trying to get some space away from your influence so that he can be his own man. That is not a bad thing. You let him have these friends so he feels like he is in control, so he lets you control him more. He can't know that these friends are letting you have more control, so don't have direct contact with these new friends.

Sledge1984: Let these new friends be like an outlet for him. I have my Kenpo to relieve myself, but you've told us that he watches a lot of sports, which may be how he escapes.

Amy1979: I thought he was escaping with me.

John2010: Right, but I hate to say this, and don't take it the wrong way, he needs to escape from you from time to time. These new friends of his, you said that he met them in a bar. Why do you think he was going to a bar? You did say you liked that these new friends are doing things with him outside of the bar and you like that, but they don't include you.

Rick1982: Maybe those new friends will stop him from becoming that drunk that you don't want him to become.

Amy1979: I just think that they are drinking someplace else.

Sledge1984: Well, it is better to be drinking with friends than to be drinking alone.

John2010: That's right, and I'm speaking from experience. Amy, what I'm saying is that letting him have some freedom on your terms gives you more control. Don't let him see it that way.

Amy1979: Right. So letting him spend time with these new friends away from me will give me more control of the time we do spend together.

Rick1982: During the times you spend together, you two can talk about his new friends and what they are doing together.

Sledge1984: Right, you did tell us that he doesn't like talking about work, so you do most of the talking as most women do.

Amy1979: So I should let him have these friends so that we have more to talk about. Okay, I see that if he has other friends, then we may be able to talk more, and I can start to talk with him about deeper issues.

John2010: Yes, but you need to take it slowly. You need to show interest in these new friends and their family and then talk about yours. Make it seem like he brought it up.

Rick1982: Yeah, I hate it when my wife start a conversation about one thing and then she changes it to what she really wants to talk about. I think that was one of the problems we had. When I found out about what was going on at work, I approached her in a totally different way and we talked about some deep issues as you say.

John2010: I think what we all should get out of this week is that communication does matter. It's not just that you talk; it is how and what you talk about.

Sledge1984: Right, and that I need to find out what to talk about with my sis. I mean, I thought I knew her well enough, but you guys are showing me an entirely different aspect of how to control our relationship.

John2010: That's what we are here for. That is why these meetings are important, and write the post about your week and how it's different from last week.

Sledge1984: I got it. I need to write a longer post and with new details. My eyes are getting tired from all of this reading. I'll see you next week.

Amy1979: I hope you can't see me. I mean, my camera isn't on…

John2010: Night, all.

John saved all of the posts and rereads them then writes three letters with details about each relationship. He attached the three letters into three separate e-mails that started with this message:

Dear Friends,

Our second meeting was very helpful to me. I hope it was more helpful to you all. I can't emphasize how important it is to write details about the people you want to change. You need to find and write about the people that they are close to for next week, so we can find how changing them will change the person who you want to change. Next week I hope to find you all there with new updated posts.
Your friend,
John

Friday's Meeting

Friday night at nine, John logged in to the work relations group to find Jill and Sally chatting about how Jill had found something to talk about with her coworkers. John could see that Sally was not relating with Jill's troubles because of their ages, but John skimmed through their two posts, which were both long. Timmy and Bill logged in soon after John starts skimming through the second post. The girls stopped chatting to read the two boys' posts.

After John finished skimming all four posts, he found that Timmy and Sally were discussing how to get ahead at work.

Timmy1982: I already had the idea of becoming closer to the men at work to get ahead at the job, but I'm not too into male bonding.

Sally1974: Timmy, you did join those men in what you told us about last week, right?

Timmy1982: It wasn't as fun as I thought, but I made some connections that may help me out with getting ahead. I just need to find out how.

Sally1974: There is that one man that you said was a head manager.

Timmy1982: He isn't a manager from my department.

Bill4267: Timmy, all of the heads talk, so if you get close with one, then he can give good credits for you to move on up.

Jill1959: It's all about making new connections.

John2010: That's right, but you need to make the right connections. From what I read, this guy sounds like he would be a good one to get to know.

Timmy1982: I did talk more with him than the other guys last weekend. I think it was because he wasn't as interested in the show.

Sally1974: That is actually a great way to connect. It is easier to connect with someone's dislikes than their likes.

John2010: But from what I read, this man has spent time with these other guys before, so you don't want to challenge these guys.

Jill1959: I have made that mistake before in my youth, and you don't want to disturb a formed friendship.

Bill4267: I've been reading how you guys have been going on about making a connection. I agree, but shouldn't Timmy be sure to make the right kind of connection first?

John2010: Right, but he has done that. Even if he doesn't think he has made a big connection, these new friends think that they're tight. Timmy, you want to keep this connection going with all of these guys, but be there to talk with the manager. If you alienate the others, just one, you may lose the connection to the manager and the entire group.

Sally1974: You want to find the guy who this man connects with the most and you'll learn how to affect this man from the third person.

Timmy1982: Okay, I see that, but I want to affect my head manager.

Jill1959: Yeah, if this man has a good view on you, then when your head asks about you, you'll get a good review.

John2010: That's right, so, Timmy, why don't you write a page about what happened on your outing with these four guys? Jill, I saw how you have connected with your coworkers and it sounds like you've started a group of your own.

Jill1959: I guess, but I half think that they are making fun of me.

Bill4267: Yes, I got that from your post, but you shouldn't view the attention you're getting like that. My nephew is somewhat of a class clown and he's gotten in trouble for it. He has told me that he does it to make even the people who are just laughing at him like him. I know, and I said that, but he said that he has made unlikely friends this way that aren't just laughing at him. That it makes him feel like a popular kid, but he also knows that he's not popular, but it's how he feels that matters.

John2010: That is a good point. As I wrote somewhere, it's not how you think they feel that matters, because how you think is very different than how your coworkers may think.

Jill1959: I've found that is true, but that just makes me think I'm old.

Sally1974: Jill, you may be older, but that is not the reason that you have different views on life, how to act, what's fun, and how to respond to others. It's just the experiences you've had and the experiences your coworkers have had.

Timmy1982: Don't let your experiences stop you from enjoying new ones.

John2010: Right, don't let actions hurt you just because you don't understand them.

Amy1979: Jill, you have to get to know your coworkers better so that you can enjoy their company.

John2010: Hi, Amy, glad you could join us. Amy is from the Family group and she was at Monday's meeting also. Bill, it looks like you have connected with the two that you wanted to.

Bill4267: Yes, and we've become friends outside of work too. Like with Timmy's group, there is one guy that they hang out with that I don't like, but it is this guy that would help me if he gave a good review. I think he is acting depressed and withdrawn because of his wife.

Amy1979: That's my group. On Wednesdays you could join us and you may get some insights on how this guy is being affected.

John2010: Right, he may have a controlling wife. Wink, wink.

Bill4267: It sounds like it is his wife that he's having problems with.

Amy1979: Very funny, but if you have a wife, then you could try to relate with him.

Bill4267: I hate hearing people rag on their wives, because they usually get carried away and I ask why are they married. You don't want me in that group 'cause I've been divorced twice.

Sally1974: I don't think you'll get a good review if you get this guy to divorce his wife. But, Bill, you could save this guy's marriage by letting him know how your marriages got messed up.

Bill4267: Right, but, Sally, I see that your boss isn't taking you any more seriously.

Jill1959: Sally, I can relate to that problem, but I think for a different reason. As John told me, it may not be the reasons we think, so I think you should get to know your bosses better.

Amy1979: Sally, I read your post and I think you are discriminated upon, because of how you look. I think you should sue for all you can get.

Sally1974: No kidding, but I like this job and I want to change how they all see me. Jill, I guess you are right, but I'm not sure about going about that.

John2010: Yes, if you like this job, then you'll need to change how your boss sees you and how the manager of your division treats you. That may be hard, but you should find what these people like to do when they aren't working. Talk to their friends to see what company they like to keep.

Amy1979: Then you can act like them, right? Sally, we have talked about this issue in the friends group, and I know that you don't want to change. If these were your friends that you wanted to see you differently, I would think that you shouldn't need to change.

Sally1974: Right, because friends should accept you for who you are. At work I would change for the money, but I just want to be more looked up to.

Timmy1982: Girls, now you're saying what we all want. I think what John is getting at is for us to find the one person that we need to make see us differently so that everyone does. I just reread your posts, and it looks like you have told us your views on the people that you need to change. Now you need to get the other people's views on them better. I just get your view that your boss is too old to change and Jill's manager is just a yes man.

John2010: That's right. Sally, you need to find out what their friends think of them, not just your friends. Yes, Timmy, I want all of us to write a third-eye view of the people that we are describing in our posts. I have written an e-mail to each person from the other meetings with these views that they may not see.

Timmy1982: John, do you want us to write a review on each other's posts?

John2010: I don't want to give you all too much work, but if you have written your own review of your day or week in full, then and only then you may write your own review of each other's posts. I just don't want anyone to feel overwhelmed.

Jill1959: Thanks, John. At work I sometimes feel overwhelmed by how much there is to do and if I ask someone for help, they just see that I'm too old to do my job.

John2010: Jill, that's how you see it. That may not be how the important people at your job see it. My sister is a media planner who feels overwhelmed a lot. I keep telling her that she needs to delegate the small stuff and take the time to do what she needs.

Bill4267: Yes, if it's just one thing I've learned, it is to delegate my time so that I have time for myself and that family I don't have anymore.

John2010: On that depressing note, let's end this meeting with the thought that we all need time for ourselves.

John logged out and saved the blogs and posts. Then he took the time to read each post and write a detailed response. He wrote an e-mail thanking the Work Relations group and he attached his views on their posts and what he thought they should elaborate on. As with the other two groups, John elaborated on how important it was to write a detailed review of their week so that they could see the changes. With the Work group, John did try to explain that to cause the changes at a place of work, they would have to change how they acted with their coworkers.

John was thinking about all three groups and saw how their concerns were a lot alike. He was also trying to make it look as if the butterfly affect that he is using was simpler than it is. John tried not to point out that each of these people would change themselves along the way. He put the emphasis on changing the other people around these subjects that would change their views on their lives. Yes, most of the subjects of John's experiment were coming to the conclusion that they might need to change their lives. John laughed and thought, *I hope none of them even think that I'm just using them as research for my new book.*

Next Monday

After a weekend of trying to compile the posts from the bloggers, Monday morning John decided that he would wait to start his book. John thought that he would have plenty of information about these subjects and how they'd changed their lives after two months. John just sat back and enjoyed his day, but as the day was ending John poured a cup of coffee. He needed the coffee because his eyes were falling shut, but he still needed to check on his subjects.

John liked relating to them as just subjects, so he wouldn't grow bonds that he knew would just be in his head, with these real people. He thought it would be easier to ignore those moral values that you hold so dear with friends.

The best friends are the ones in your head, but I have plenty.

John logged on to the blog and into the private room that he had set up for the friends group and found that three subjects were logged in. Two of them had been chatting about how this idea of John's had been working.

Tarry1978: Mike, it sounds like you have been discovering what these new friends of yours think of you. But as John has told us don't jump to conclusions, but find what or why these guys like you. Once you've found that out you can change the reasons and manipulate them.

Mike1991: After reading my post again, I think I was too hard on them.

John2010: The first impression usually is.

Tarry1978: Right, but, Mike, you have been hanging with these guys for a while now, so what have you changed to make these guys rag on you like that?

Mike1991: Well, I think that I'm just listening more, but how can I get them to stop it and treat me more as an equal?

John2010: Mike, that is an easy one. You just need to make it known that it's upsetting to you that these guys are treating you like that. That girl you like or one of her friends, just pull them aside and start talking about how upset these guys are making you. Don't whine or complain too much, but let it be known that you don't like it.

Anna1983: Yeah, Mike, it's like that saying, it never hurts to ask, you might just get it. I'm sure these guys are just having fun and you should be able to just take it, but then they'll never stop. If you start talking to one of the friends of this girl that they are teasing you about, and open up to her, then they may realize that there is more to like about you.

Tarry1978: Like with Jamie's friends, I just needed to say something but I don't like to complain. One of them started to complain for me, but I think he was half mocking me. I didn't let it get to me.

Alex1986: I think he was and I hate it when my friends do that, so I act like I'm about to storm off and they notice it and say sorry. I think that is what John is getting at. Helping us to find out what to do to make the changes in our relationships we want.

John2010: Yes, but just storming off sounds too juvenile. If your friends think they have to act a way to keep you, they may just let you go.

Anna1983: Right, you don't want to make it hard for your friends, but you should be able to show your emotions. Nobody likes the friend that is too emotional, though.

Tarry1978: There is an attraction to having someone like that, but, Mike, I'm sure you don't share your emotions much. John is right about talking to one of your friends or a friend's friend, not to complain but to share.

Alex1986: They're right, of course. But, Mike, now you need to think of the best person to open up to. Don't try to talk with that girl you like. Talk to the one friend who can influence the leader of the pack.

John2010: Right, or the one who can influence his girlfriend.

Mike1991: Okay, I hear you. Tarry, it sounds like what you have started with your friends is to get closer to the friends that your best friend has been hanging with more.

Tarry1978: Yeah, and I see what's attractive about them and it isn't one of their girlfriends, Mike. They have been exposing her to other things like the arts or something. We all went out for coffee and Jamie was even talking differently. She seemed happy, but I had a hard time joining the conversation.

Anna1983: That can be expected with joining new groups. Just give it time and do what John has said and engage with these new friends.

Tarry1978: Yeah, but it's just me and Jamie for life and I don't want to share her. I know that's juvenile, John, and don't tell me to let her free. I can do more with her new friends and see how it turns out.

Alex1986: You could learn why she likes these friends and try to give that to her.

Tarry1978: Oh, she likes them just because they're different. Alex, I was reading your post. It sounds like you've been interrogating your friends.

Alex1986: No, it's more like I've been listening more and interrogating my days. I've started to keep somewhat of a journal, and as I look back on my day I see how I act and my friends act. John is right about taking notes every day to see how you change and your friends change.

John2010: That's good that you got it. You just need to pay attention to what is happening and learn how to cause change. You can change your world.

Mike1991: I get it. I just have to step up to make a difference.

John2010: Don't scare me, Mike. Now, it's not that you need to act, it is how you act that matters. The smallest changes can make a big difference.

Tarry1978: That's right, the closer you are to the person, the more the little things count.

Anna1983: Yeah, but I do not want to get closer to my friend's boyfriend. I told you about Scott and how he flirts with everyone. He just annoys me, he is going out with one of my best friends and I think he cheats a lot.

John2010: Anna, that may be how he is and he's too insecure to be himself. You know, when people are always on it means that they don't like themselves. They try too hard to get people to like them, or he may just talk like that.

Mike1991: Yeah, that's how this other guy I know acts and I've noticed that he likes being the center of attention. I think he just acts out like a class clown or something. He always needed to be involved and it was too draining, so I left that crowd.

Anna1983: Yeah, I get tired around Scott. I just thought I was tired of him, but I actually get exhausted. I'll talk with Julie. She might be concerned when I tell her that I think Scott is depressed or something.

Alex1986: She might take that the wrong way.

Anna1983: I have told her that I don't like how Scott is always flirting and has to be involved with everything. Maybe if I tell her that he is showing his insecurities, that will get her attention to act. The last time I complained about him, Julie got mad.

John2010: That's why you should show concern for Scott's well-being. Don't overdo it, though. Your friend may ask herself, "Why is she so concerned about my boyfriend?"

Tarry1978: Yeah, Jamie has asked that question when I first asked her about her new friends. I guess I was interrogating her too much. That sounds right, though. When I show concern about her, she blows me off, but is talking with a mutual friend about Jamie, they may show concern also.

Mike1991: I think that's how it's done. You show a friend that you are concerned about another friend and have them take care of it.

John2010: Not exactly, but this friend can help you get to know why your other friend is acting like that. You can find a way to change how the other friend is acting by changing this friend. This friend will act in a way that may help show how troubling the other friend that you want to change is acting and can cause change.

Alex1986: Yes, but it may not be the change that you are looking for. I was telling someone about something and they took it the wrong way. That one conversation was passed along, but not how I meant it to be or wanted it to be. I was just venting, I think.

Tarry1978: Yeah, you want to be careful who you vent with and what you are venting about.

John2010: That is why you need to do research about your friends and what makes them tick. This may sound like work, but if you write about your day in detail it will come easy. It's getting late, so I'm leaving you with this thought: "How would you hustle someone you didn't know?"

Anna1983: Why would I want to trick anyone?

Tarry1978: I don't think John wants to turn us into hustlers. He's trying to get us to think of this as a game.

Anna1983: I'm not playing, I want to make my best friend understand that her boyfriend isn't right for her.

Tarry1978: Anna, maybe you don't know this friend as well as you think.

John logged off, hoping that his subjects were really understanding what he was getting at. Before John turned in, he read each post again and wrote more detailed comments about each of them. He waited until the next morning to send the e-mails to each of them with the comments he had about each post. John rereads his comments before sending the e-mails and attached his detailed responses to their posts:

My Friends,

Monday's meeting went well. I think you all are getting the idea of learning about your friends more. You should want to do this to bring you closer. I am helping you all make your relationships better by letting you know it should be easy to change them.

The last comment was to make you think of how you might profit from changing a stranger. I know you don't want to take advantage of your friends. You will profit from learning more about them, and the more you know, the easier it will be to get them to change. With posts that are more detailed, I can better comment on how you are doing. Don't take my comments harshly. If I don't know what's happening, then I may say the wrong things. Details are good and remember, it is the little things that make the difference.

Your Friend,

John

Family Group

Tuesday was going by fast and John thought that he should do some research about family matters. He knew that it was important to sound as if he knew what he was talking about. John also knew it would be better if he actually knew what to talk about for the group on Wednesday. John searched the Web on how to deal with family matters. By Tuesday night he thought he knew enough to fill a book about families with problems.

On Wednesday, John went through his daily routine for Wednesdays. As the hour crept up on John, he reviewed the posts and his comments about the Family group. He logged on to the site to find Amy and Sedge already chatting about how well things seemed to be working for them.

Amy1979: I have been listening to my husband and writing about it every night and I have realized how much I don't hear. I mean, I rarely listen to him. I always assume that I know what he is talking about.

Sledge1984: My sister is like that. She doesn't see how I've changed from how I once was. She has an image of me and can't see anything else. She thinks she knows what I'm going to do or say and acts on what she believes I am going to do.

Amy1979: Right, but what John has told us to do most of all is to listen. Taking notes really helps with listening, and reviewing your day helps.

Sledge1984: I'm not that into writing a daily journal, but looking back on this week, I wrote two pages that opened my eyes. I think Andy is gay. He was giving his friends too much attention when we hung out last Saturday and I got a gay vibe from it.

Amy1979: That's funny, but you know when you're with your friends you get close. Or are you the type that keeps his shield up all the time and gets uncomfortable when other people let it down?

Sledge1984: I thought it was just girls who did that. My wife gets too close with her friends and I thought it was just her, but maybe it's her family. Her sister noticed that the last two weekends I was hanging with them and my wife asked me why.

Amy1979: Yeah, that was funny. You wrote a long post this week.

Rick had logged in and he was reading the posts and was enjoying Sledge's post too much. John finished skimming over the three posts.

John2010: I've read that all of you have made progress. I can see that you all have grasped the concept, but I can't encourage you all enough to write weekly journals. That is why I want to have these weekly meetings with you. My first insights on your week are that you have all found how important it is to listen. Rick, I read how you asked your wife if you could get to know her friends, and I just shook my head. It sounds like the honest way was a good way with her, but you gave her too much control. I'm glad you didn't tell her about us, and I think you can use this honesty thing to your advantage.

Amy1979: Didn't you tell us not to be funny?

John2010: Being honest is a way to show trust and to give someone a misgiven confidence in you if it's used in the right way. I know that you don't want to use or trick your loved once.

Amy1979: I don't, I just want Jim to include me with his friends. I want to stay a part of his life.

Sledge1984: Amy, from what I've read from your posts, you are high maintenance. Don't take that the wrong way. You like to have the control in a way that can be draining at times.

Amy1979: HA, I don't like it when he goes out alone.

John2010: Right, what Sledge is saying is that if your husband needs time away from you… That is okay! If you want to feel like a part of it, then talk about his day or evening with his friends. I emphasize his friends and let him tell the story. You can comment about his friends, just don't tell him what to do with his friends.

Amy1979: I heard that last week and I did it, but yes, thinking back, you're right, I did try too hard to become a part of his outing, after the fact. I see, I guess, but I don't see how it will give me more control.

Rick1982: I see it. I have talked with some of my wife's coworkers and I found why she has been acting distant, and I told you that we talked last week. I got her to open up and I told her that I'm here to listen. She started talking gibberish to my ears at first. I listened and I made some comment that I didn't really notice I made, but she did. Then she asked me what I thought, so I told her and she listened.

Sledge1984: That talking and listening thing really works?

Rick1982: Yes. I mean, I feel like I'm a part of what is going on at her work if she lets me give her advice, which is me telling her what to do, I guess.

John2010: That is good, Rick, but, Amy, as Rick said, giving advice is telling someone what you think they should do. It's how you give that advice that matters. Give the least advice to get your idea across and let your husband put it together. Your husband or wife won't even know you just told them what to do.

Sledge1984: I have noticed that with my wife's family. Her mother and father are good with that. They know just what to say to persuade their children to do it their way. I thought it was just because it was family. I was out with her father last weekend and he talked a friend of his into something. It was scary how he did it so easily, looking back on it. I have to watch him.

Rick1982: Sledge, you should have written more about that. You just said that you needed to get away from Andy. I see that the small events that happen in our lives should be looked at closer. My wife changed because of something that I thought would have had little effect.

John2010: That's it, just changing a small thing can have a big effect.

Amy1979: Right, but changing how I talk to my husband is a big thing.

John2010: You shouldn't see it that way. Yes, watching what you say is big, but just don't say as much. I thought you all would know something about social interacting. I'm not going to give too detailed advice on this because it changes with everyone. I do encourage you all to read up on it. You can find this information on-line.

Sledge1984: Yeah, Amy, the whole concept is to listen more. I know it may be hard not to talk, but gab with your friends and listen with your husband.

Rick1982: Right, you know how your husband needs space or time for himself. Well, so do you.

John2010: That's right, you all need time for yourself away from this person you are worrying about.

Amy1979: I don't want to spend time away from my husband. I spend too much time away from him when he's at work.

Sledge1984: That's what I mean, by you being the type of girl that needs too much control over your husband. I mean, you like knowing what your husband does, how he does it, and who he does it with. That can be draining.

Rick1982: You may be pushing him away. You need time for yourself to give him time for himself.

John2010: Right, Amy, you need to find something you like to do by yourself or with a friend. Something you enjoy without your husband. I know that you want to change something about your husband, but finding your own thing will help. From what I read, these two guys are right and you should listen to them, because it doesn't sound like your husband is going to say it.

Amy1979: So what you're all saying is that I may be pushing my husband away. I hear you all, but, John, why do I need to find something to do away from my husband?

John2010: It's good for anyone to have something they can do that they enjoy like a hobby. Reading or watching TV is something someone does because they don't have a hobby to keep them busy. Don't get me wrong. A movie buff or a book reviewer is a very entertaining hobby. A hobby using your hands or one that gets you out is what I'm thinking would be good. Your husband needs to see you keeping yourself busy so that he doesn't think he has to keep you busy.

Amy1979: Okay, I have some ideas, but how is me keeping myself busy going to help me get my husband to do what I want?

John2010: Looking like you have something to do is relaxing for you and your husband. It makes it look as if you have something to do other than waiting for him to find out what he's up to. It makes it look like he is interrupting you when he asks "How are you?". When you ask him what he has been doing, it won't seem that you've been waiting to ask that very question. If he makes a short comment, then you may need to persist but not too strongly. Make him feel like he is telling a story, not being interrogated.

Sledge1984: I know exactly what you mean. My wife keeps asking questions before I've even finished answering the first one.

Rick1982: My wife is more subtle, but sometimes I just ask one question and she goes on and on.

Amy1979: My friend at work does that and it can get annoying.

John2010: Amy, why don't you join us on Friday with work relations? We can talk about keeping them separate from home. Sledge, I think you need to be more open with your wife and find out more about her brother. Rick, it sounds good, but don't let your wife find out that you've been checking up on her at work.

Sledge1984: Yeah, Rick. If she finds out you've been spying, then that honest thing will crash.

Amy1979: I will be here on Friday and I'll pick up on some of those hobbies I had at college.

Rick1982: See you all next week, so to say, or type…

John logged off, rereads each of the posts, and wrote comments on each one. John's comments were more specific now that he knew more of the stories:

Dear Friends,

I have gained more details about each of your situations and made better comments about your troubles. These weekly posts are to help you gain a better view of your situations. My view and the views of the others from the blog are to give you a third-eye view. This week's posts had more details about each situation. In any situation, good social skills are necessary, so I encourage you to search on-line for information about developing your own family relations skills. I would like to see that each week the details in your post are more in-depth. Remember, these posts are to help you along the way of gaining what you want.
Your Friend,
John

Work Group

John had looked for information about work relationships, but he just found that it was mostly the same conflicts as he found with families. By Friday he was doing the same routine he did most Fridays, but as the hour was rounding down, he rereads last week's posts.

After John had logged in to the blog, he was surprised to find that the new posts were showing how these subjects were using this Butterfly Affect already.

Jill1959: Sally, I just read your post and it sounds as if you're getting some respect. All you did was help the right coworker and she gabbed about how you helped her. Now other coworkers are looking towards you for help.

Sally1974: Yeah, they are looking at me differently. It was an accident that I helped that girl. When other people looked towards me for help, I acted more confident. I think looking like you know what you're doing really is most important.

John2010: Didn't I tell you guys that? Well, yes, I think the people at your job weren't showing you the respect that you wanted, Sally, because of how you carry yourself. If you look confident, then you'll gain more respect than if you look unsure about yourself.

Sally1974: The people who I look up to at work just look so confident in what they're doing. I don't think I have it in me to look like them, but being more sure of myself helps.

Jill1959: Yes, when a young man at work started helping me before I even asked, I got annoyed but just for an instant. I told him that I could do it, but he could help me out with something else. Now he asks before helping and I think he told other people that I almost bit his head off. I didn't want to come across like that, but I feel that other coworkers are treating me as if I'm stronger.

Bill4267: Sometimes you need to bark a little to get the respect. I think they just fear you now. Fear is good if it's used in the right way.

Jill1959: I don't want to scare people. I guess to make people think before taking me for granted is good. I think that is kind of what I want.

Timmy1982: Yes, they may fear you for a day, but they'll respect you for at least a week. You can build on that by showing them that confidence Sally now has. Bill, it really looks like you have made the right connections now, finding a bar that a number of the head managers from your office building go to after work.

Bill4267: I don't know that I'm making connections with them all, but I'm in the same bar. This bar is in the other direction from my house. That is why I didn't have the connections I wanted. The guys that I went with introduced me to a table of men who work on my floor and we all started talking. Oh, I listened a lot too.

Timmy1982: Bill, it looks like you have found the connection that you need to affect your heads. There is that gathering next weekend that I'm getting involved with. I'll try to find the group from my floor and make the right connections.

John2010: That's right, Timmy. I read that you are helping out those guys with a presentation at that party. That is how you get recognized. Jill, I like how you are trying to get a group of coworkers to join you in an activity.

Jill1959: I don't know if it's a group, but at lunch I sit at a table with these girls that talk while I eat. That is just what happens, but this week I listened and heard one of the girls say that she was into collecting antique dolls. Her friends laughed.

Bill4267: I would too. One of my ex-wives collected old stuff. That kept her busy and out of my hair, but even that became too much of a nuisance.

Amy1979: That's your problem. Collecting things is a great hobby.

John2010: I was wondering where you were. I asked Amy to join us tonight to discuss work relationships. I'm sure you all know that work relationships are different than relationships you have at home or with your friends.

Bill4267: Amy, you are right that I did have problems accepting the things my wives did without me.

Sally1974: I thought that comment from Amy was rather demeaning, but I guess it makes us think of how our home life affects us at work.

John2010: Yes, and vice versa. Bill and Amy are a lot alike. They both like to be in control. Amy is trying to work on her relationship with her husband. Amy was saying how annoying it can get to listen to someone gab about something that she isn't interested in. Now, listening is good and when anyone gabs too much, they are excited or they are hiding something.

Bill4267: Both of my wives talked too much and they were saying the same thing over and over. Oh, they weren't each saying the same thing, it's just that they tended to repeat themselves.

Timmy1982: I don't know about your wives, but at work it gets annoying when my boss keeps repeating himself. I just think that's because he doesn't know what to say.

Jill1959: I have friends who do that, but I think they are just old and don't get enough to do.

John2010: Yes, keeping yourself busy is important. That is why we were talking about finding hobbies on Wednesday. Bill, what hobbies do you have?

Bill4267: I play cards with my friends once a month.

John2010: Right, so during the week you worked or spent time with your wife.

Bill4267: I spent time at the bar.

John2010: There's no problem going out with friends and having a drink, but if you drink alone, you should find out why.

Jill1959: I like wine, so I have a glass every night and I'm alone.

John2010: If it's one glass, that is fine.

Bill4267: I would drink more than that and it was because I didn't want to go home to my wife.

John2010: You needed something to go home to, and if you had a hobby, then you would have that to do. Finding a hobby is a preventative measure. Find something you like, as in a sport or an object, and put more into it. Don't let this hobby interfere with work—it's just to give you something to do outside of work.

Sally1974: It's so you don't get too absorbed by your work and it's a good way to connect at work by sharing these hobbies that I'm sure you all will find. I have to go, so I'll see you all next week.

Amy1979: Sally is right. There are a lot of hobbies that may interest you. If you are interested in anything, then it's likely to find someone that is interested in it too. They may not be who you think, so one thing that John has told us is not to let our assumptions hold us back.

John2010: Yes, that is what holds most of us back. The fact that we aren't open to different people. So keep your ears opened and you might be surprised, what you hear. If you have trouble interacting with strangers, then I would suggest that you get information about developing your social skills.

Jill1959: John, I was taught not to speak with strangers, let alone be social with them.

John2010: Jill, we aren't children, and to get ahead in life you may just need to make new friends. Now, I like that you've found a hobby to share with some girls at work. I hope you find more people to join this group, so don't hesitate just because you don't know them. Now, I'm talking about strangers at work. That shouldn't be dangerous to you. If you go on an outing with these new friends, then you may need to put that guard up with strangers.

Timmy1982: That's right, these strangers at work may help you find the right connections to cause change in your life.

Bill4267: Yeah, that's right. The guys I found a connection with are helping me find the right connections and they don't even know it.

Amy1979: I'm trying to connect with my husband better, and, Bill, it doesn't sound like you will be any help with that.

Bill4267: What I think John asked you here to find is what can happen if you don't listen to your husband more and make it easier for him. I avoided spending time with my wives, and our relationships just fell apart.

John2010: Yes, as I've told you, a hobby is good to have to keep yourself busy, so your spouse doesn't feel like they have to make it their business to keep you busy. That may not be said right. If you look busy, then that takes pressure off the people around you. If they want you for something, making them feel like they are interrupting you puts them on the defense.

Jill1959: I don't want to make people feel like they need to defend themselves. I think I get what you're saying, John. If you look like you're doing nothing, then people will think, "What's she up to?" If they feel like they are interrupting you, then that puts them in an apologetic mode.

John2010: I couldn't have said it better. It's easier to talk to a passive person than a person with a purpose. Thank you. Great posts this week.

Amy1979: Wait, John. And, Bill, I'm afraid that my husband is doing what you did, Bill. I'm afraid that I'm pushing him away.

Bill4267: After both of my wives found that I was spending too much time away from them, well, they just pushed me away even more by showing too much interest in what I was doing. They started to kind of interrogate me.

Amy1979: John told me about not being too aggressive and letting my husband tell the story.

John2010: That's right. You should investigate, but not directly. You should ask his friends and coworkers, but not best friends, about how he's doing. This goes for work relations too. Ask around about the person you are trying to change, but don't get too close.

John signed off, he rereads each post that was more detailed with views of the people the subjects were working with. John could see that these people wanted to get ahead in their jobs, but mostly they just wanted to be appreciated more.

John wrote them all the standard e-mail with notes about their posts. He even wrote Amy an email:

Hi, Amy,
  I wanted to make sure that you understood why I thought you would have benefitted from Friday's group. I think that it is important to keep work and home separate. I thought that Bill would help you see that and help with how to deal with your husband. He did added a purpose to listening more and letting your husband tell the story of his day, how he wishes. I'm going to ask Bill to join our family group, because I don't know how big his families have been, but he may have insights for the group.
Your Friend,
John

Monday's Friends

Over the weekend, John didn't want to think about his project, so he went out to a museum. He liked reading the displays at the museum, but they didn't take him any place new. John finished his outings at the library reading about far-off places and imaginary adventures.

On Monday morning, John went through his normal routine until he finished his lunch. Then he reviewed the posts and his responses of the Friends group. John just shook his head and took a gulp of his coffee.

As the hour came, John logged on to the blog to find that all four of his subjects were logged on. Two subjects were chatting about how their lives had changed in such a short time and how the little things really counted.

Anna1983: I just told Pattie that I thought Scott looked depressed and Pattie said, he always looks like that. So I asked, Why is he always depressed? Pattie gave me a strange look, went to Scott, and they talked for some time.

Mike1991: I'm sure that got her thinking. I just saw that Brad was thinking before the others joined us, so I talked to him. He was saying that it was nothing, but I told him about how someone was annoying me and he related. Brad actually said how Jay annoys him and I said that I hate it when Jay dismisses me from the conversation and overlooks me. Then Brad went on how Jay used to do that a lot with him until he had a fit and screamed at him.

Anna1983: Well, I think you better be sure that these friends will stay your friends before going off.

Mike1991: I don't go off like Brad can, but I didn't have to do anything. Brad is one of those characters that speaks his mind. He just told Jay that I told him that he's pissing me off. Now, I never said that, but that's how Brad translated what I said.

Anna1983: I have an overdramatic friend like that too, and she is too literal about everything. I just watch what I say to her.

Tarry1978: I used to have a friend like that but he was just too exhausting.

John2010: Yes, friends that act overdramatic can be exhausting. There are some people that like having a friend like that in their group of friends. If you know who they are, then you can use them as Mike did.

Mike1991: Wait, I didn't mean for that to happen. I wouldn't even have talked to Brad if I knew he was going to tell Jay like that!

John2010: Right, but you need to find the dynamic of your group of friends and learn how to use it.

Tarry1978: Jamie's new friends are all overdramatic, but they are all arty types. Most of my friends are down-to-earth and aren't so dramatic. This weekend I went out with Jamie and two of her new friends. I could see how different they are from our usual friends, and they were fun for a night out.

Alex1986: I can't stand how some of my friends are totally different when we go out. I mean, yes, some are dramatic about some things always, but when we are out they sometimes take it too far.

John2010: That's the thing you need to look for in each group. You need to find the most dramatic and the most down-to-earth friend, and you can use them to affect the entire group. When they change, the group dynamic changes.

Anna1983: I thought we were investigating for the leader of our group and the bottom of our totem pole.

John2010: You should know them also. I just wanted you all to take a better look at your group of friends. After you have found these four people that form your group dynamic, then you can change your group.

Anna1983: I just wanted to change Scott.

Mike1991: Right, but if I could change the group at will, I would.

Tarry1978: Now, Mike, you are friends with these people for a reason, and if you change the group too much, you may lose that reason.

John2010: That's right, but you can't do too much damage yet. I mean, you don't even know these friends of yours yet. I don't just mean Mike, but if Mike knew Brad, then he would have known what he would do with the information that he gave him. Alex, from your long post I see that you have found where each of your friends stand.

Alex1986: Well, not each of them, just the ones in the group that I want to change. I don't mean to brag, but I've got a lot of friends. They are in groups like Work Friends, Neighbors, School Friends, and Beach Buddies. I'm starting to go out more with friends from school, and that is the group dynamic that I'm trying to change.

Anna1983: That's a lot. I have enough trouble with the friends I grew up with.

Alex1986: Well, when I was young I moved a lot because my dad's work changed a lot. My uncle has a house at the beach that was my only constant house as a child. I guess my beach buddies are the ones I grew up with, three months a year.

Tarry1978: I guess I'm trying to change or join Jamie's new friends, so I should find the dynamics of that group of friends.

Mike1991: I found that my group of friends has subgroups that you were telling us about last week. I was focusing on the main group of friends, but I was thinking that I should find a subgroup. The subgroups that are formed by the dramatics and the more somber people or the not so dramatics.

John2010: That is right, the subgroups that are formed are there to get away from the big group dynamic. In other words, aren't there some friends that you are just more comfortable with? Well, those are the people that you can be yourself with and relax easier with. Maybe you don't need to change your group of friends, you just need to find one or two friends who let you be yourself.

Tarry1978: I thought I found her, but now she got these new friends.

Alex1986: You are the only one that thinks you are the center of the world. That's a good thing! I used to have a girlfriend that was too clingy and I was glad when that summer was over.

Anna1983: Right, but, Tarry, you may want to look closer at your relationship with Jamie. You two may be falling further apart than you realize. My friend's new boyfriend is what I thought was pulling us apart, which they always do. After I have taken a closer look at Pattie's life, I see that she has changed, but so have I.

John2010: That's right, the change that you want may be you. This is for all of you to find out for yourselves. Now, if you find this to be true, I don't want you to give up on this project. Like Mike wants to join a new group of friends and have a changing impact on them, so he can make the best out of his new friends. You all can do this with any type of friends.

Alex1986: As I have been taking a closer look at all of my friends, the beach buddies have been the ones that have changed the most. With them I've seen how I have changed also, because there are two of them that I've been friends with forever, and they didn't change, but I have. I have other friends there, so we still hang out.

Mike1991: Well, like John has pointed out, I'm looking to make new friends or at least make a better impression on them. Like with Brad, that time we talked did bring us closer, I guess, and I'm seeing how he makes a bigger impression on these friends than I thought.

Tarry1978: Mike, it sounds like he's just dramatic and it sounds as if you aren't, so don't become overdramatic in a day. That may turn your new friends away, but you can show them what you feel strongly about in your life and share those emotions. Jamie's new friends do that too much, so all I'm saying is it's okay to show strong feelings, but not with everything.

Alex1986: Right, I have other friends that are fun when the beach races are running, but when there aren't any races they are just boring. What I'm thinking is to find something to start with, but don't base your friendship on it.

John2010: Yes, I think I've mentioned that it's good to find something in common like a hobby to make a friendship closer. Sharing dislikes is a good way to open up any relationship, because most people love complaining. Some people like keeping things closed in and don't like to share emotions and may not like hearing yours. I'm thinking that you should know the person and be sure that he/she won't be turned off, before you share.

Mike1991: That's right!

Anna1983: I think I know Pattie good, but yes, I want to be closer again. I could try to bring back some old things we used to do.

Tarry1978: Why did you stop doing those things?

Mike1991: Right, you must have stopped them for a reason, so make sure she won't reject them.

Anna1983: Well, Pattie has had a number of boyfriends that have changed her each time.

Alex1986: Have you had a boyfriend that hasn't changed you?

Anna1983: Well, I married my high school sweetheart that Pattie keeps reminding me of, when I try to make her see how bad her choices of boyfriends are.

John2010: Does Pattie ever speak badly of him?

Anna1983: No, but he's great!

Mike1991: Is she jealous?

Anna1983: NO! She has plenty. I just complain too much. I see that's how I've changed. I need to stop that and try to help her make the right choices. I think we need to spend more time together and become like we were.

John2010: That's good, Anna, but remember it will never be like it was. Tarry, that goes for you too, but it sounds like you both don't want to lose a friendship that may be slipping away. Look, listen, and find things to do together. That's how we have to end it today. Remember, you all need to look at your friendships with a third-eye perspective to find truths.

John signed off because his stomach was rumbling. He went to the kitchen in search of something to eat. While John ate, he was thinking about the relationships of his subjects. He was seeing how each group wanted the same thing. Except, the family group needed more attention than John thought. John wrote the subjects of the friends group all an e-mail with a story he read about while doing his research:

Dear Friends,
I am happy to see that your posts have more details in them, and the smallest detail can be the most important. I read a story that I think you should all hear my explanation for it.

The story begins with a big glass jar that gets filled with golf balls. Is this jar full? Then you add small marbles and shake the jar until the empty spots are filled in. Is this jar full? And then you add a bag of sand and shake the jar again. Is this jar full? You sit down and pick up a beer. You look at the jar. You pour two beers Into the jar, which changes the sand. Now it's full, is it?

The jar was full of golf balls, which represent the most important things in your life. The marbles represent the important things that you can do without. The sand represents the everyday happenings. There's always room for two beers.

In this venture I want you to see the sands and see how the small things matter. The sand adds weight and meaning to your life. If the sands change, then your life will change without you knowing. This venture we are all on is to change the people around us to make them see us as we wish. If you haven't realized it by now, it is the sands that we are trying to change.

We need to learn to read the sands in our lives and the sands in the lives we are trying to affect. It is easy to change a sand here or there that will affect the one golf ball of your life you want to change. That's right, you are the two beers here changing YOUR Life.
Your friend,
John

A Strong Family

John had started to compile each subject's information into separate files. He saved each file to a subfolder titled "changing." This folder was in the book's folder that backed up the new or changed files automatically every day. John was working on building these files most of the day on Tuesday. He did use the shortcut commands to find and copy this information. John hated busywork, and that was all this was to him. He sat at his computer complaining to himself, until realizing that his complaining was just making it take longer.

John soon finished compiling the information about each subject and his or her problems. He tried to read them through, but he just saw the stupidity of the complaints and stopped himself. Wednesday came and went until John saw the time and logged on to the blog site. He read tonight's posts about the subjects and decided how he was to approach the group.

John2010: This family group is working out better than I expected. I have read your previous posts today, and as I read tonight's I see that you are grasping how the little things count. Most of you have constructed a list about your friends. I am glad to find that some of you are looking deeper to find what makes those things important to you.

I hope you all are seeing how other people see these people that you want to change.

Amy1979: Yes, I have been talking with Jim's friends at work to get their views on him. They haven't informed me of anything that I didn't already know.

John2010: What you want to find out is why he's how he is. If he acts the same way with the people at work as he acts with you, then I would want to find out why.

Sledge1984: I wouldn't want to hear that my wife treats the guys at work the same way as she treats me.

Amy1979: No, I don't mean that...

Rick1982: Right, but I would hope that my wife would feel different at work or with friends than Crista feels around me.

Amy1979: Oh, Jim has new friends at that bar. Maybe he's trying something different, or is he trying to get away from something?

John2010: I have a friend that got new friends that his girlfriend didn't like. My friend liked hanging out with these new friends, because they were different and he could be somebody different with them.

Rick1982: Right, some people need an escape to relieve themselves from the stresses of their lives. I'm not suggesting he's trying to escape from you, but it sounds like Jim's looking for a change. John has told us to find a hobby to keep us busy, so that our idle hands don't cause trouble. Well, I can see why you don't want Jim to have idle hands at a bar, so why don't you two join a club?

Sledge1984: Find something he enjoyed doing at college and do it with him. Like join a bowling team or racquetball.

John2010: Yes, a good way to lessen the tension is sports or an activity that you both enjoy. Drinking is a good way to relieve tension, but I don't know if you want to take Jim wine tasting.

Amy1979: I'll make a list of the activities he used to like doing.

Rick1982: I did that when I was looking at my brother. When I was putting my wife's list together, I added the things that my brother used to like doing. I guess those activities helped make him into the person that he is today.

John2010: Exactly, the way to change someone is to find out what has changed them in the past. You do this by taking apart their lives. I hope you are all realizing that you do this by looking at these people with a third-eye perspective.

Sledge1984: Yeah, I am doing that, I think, but why would a stranger know more than I would about my sister?

Amy1979: I think we have to remove ourselves from the situation and take a look. I have investigated my husband's activities at work from coworkers who don't socialize much with him outside of the job. What I've learned wasn't surprising, but their respect for him was. I mean how they saw him.

John2010: Right, don't think you can just detach yourself from your relationship and see them as others do. You need to actually talk to other people about them, but watch out for any overemphasizing. When you talk about someone, I'm sure you emphasize what you like about them.

Rick1982: Well, yeah, but how do we know when other people are overemphasizing?

Sledge1984: Jeff, my wife's father is a straight talker who never overemphasizes unless he means to. I think I've learned to see when he does that, but if I wasn't looking I'd be fooled. I am spending more time with him and Andy. Jen and my sister think I'm just trying to get on their good side. Jen seems happy about it.

Rick1982: Okay, so I just have to look for it. I have been looking at Crista and her family closer, and I have seen some things about them that I haven't realized before. I don't have anybody like Sledge. His father-in-law seems to be a good example. From what I read, Jeff seems a bit controlling and I don't like people like that.

John2010: You can be your own man. Just see more of what's going on around you, and how the people you care about react. Once you know how to make these people react a certain way, then you can have them react in your favor.

Amy1979: I think that is what Rick doesn't like. When people control how you are going to act.

Sledge1984: Right, but it's you who is doing the controlling. I don't like being controlled either, and when I notice that I'm being directed, I do the other thing, whatever it is.

John2010: Sledge, it's never good to act in spite, because if someone sees that in you, then guess what… They see an easy way to control you. Amy, from what I've read, you like being in control. You just need to do it better. Jim seems to have realized when you are too demanding. Taking time to watch and listen will give you the ability to gain more control. If it's done right, he won't even know it and may like it…

Rick1982: I've been finding new things about people that I thought I knew as I made the lists. Now I think I'm understanding how to use them. I see that Joe likes golf, but I don't, so we don't play golf together. Now if I want him to understand me, I should use simple golf metaphors to keep his attention. I do understand golf, I'm just not interested in it, but using references to it will help with my relationship with Joe.

Amy1979: I have noticed how your posts have changed. Are you getting along with your brother better?

Rick1982: We have been sending e-mails and he called me, which was surprising.

John2010: When I read that, I thought you were seeing an effect from my idea. Then I read on, but at least he did want to talk.

Rick1982: Right, we talked for about ten minutes and not just about that outing.

Amy1979: You told us that in your post, but what did you talk about? I know you don't have to tell us, but you said that you use golf metaphors.

Rick1982: Yes, I wouldn't have thought of doing that if it wasn't for this group. I made a list about Joe and what his likes and dislikes are. This list helped me see what John is telling us about. How you talk to someone is as important as what you talk about. I couldn't figure how I was supposed to know how to talk to my brother. It just took time to look at Joe and see what he's all about now. He really hasn't changed that much.

Sledge1984: I really am seeing my sister differently now that I've taken a closer look. Oh, and you are right about Barbs father, but I think he just likes having control of his family. He is good at reading people, but when we are out he doesn't so much control everyone, but just says the right things.

Amy1979: Right, he says the things that get people to do as he wishes.

Sledge1984: Wow, Amy, he doesn't make people do anything.

John2010: That's right, Amy, it looks like you have been too demanding with your husband. Jeff just knows how to control people by not being demanding.

Amy1979: Right, and that's what you've said I have to learn. I have found things to keep busy, so Jim doesn't think he needs to keep me entertained. That has stopped me from worrying too much. I keep myself busy.

John2010: Yes, keeping busy is a good way of passing the time and it stops you from worrying about something you're just putting too much thought into. Last week I emphasized that you all find a hobby, so you have something to keep yourself busy. That takes a lot off the shoulders of people around you. Who is around you the most? Your family, and they worry about you more than you realize, so if you look like you are busy, then they don't pay you any mind. When they want you for something, they are already asking for your forgiveness. This is a great way to lead into an unwanted conversation with them.

Rick1982: Why would I want to have an unwanted conversation?

Sledge1984: It's not you who doesn't want it!

John2010: "Oh, excuse me, am I interrupting you?" "***" Then you ask, "Well, how did that *** work out?"

Rick1982: Oh, I get it!

Amy1979: Yeah, but Jim is too hesitant to interrupt me sometimes. I had to stop him from hovering around me.

Bill4267: That's right blame it on him. My wives didn't like including me in some of their activities, and that just made me feel unwelcome. I learned not to interrupted them at times.

John2010: Bill, glad you joined us, but don't attack each other.

Bill4267: I'm not I'm just trying to help Amy see that there may be a reason that Jim is scared of her.

Amy1979: He's not scared.

John2010: Amy and Bill you two need to listen to each other. Didn't I mention that you all should find something to do with your husband or wife? Well, with that I should be saying good night.

John logged off, but Amy and Bill chatted about what to do, so Amy's marriage doesn't end up like Bills have. As John rereads tonight's posts he was happy with how this group was turning out. He wrote a longer e-mail for each of the subjects of the family group. John tried to give more specific instructions, but he stopped himself. *I don't want to be telling these people what to do. I just want to help them see for themselves how to d*o it. John did add the story of the jar of life to this e-mail to help them with their lists about their families.

Dear Friends,

I am happy with your progress up to today and it looks like you are starting to use some of the things you've learned. Now you should try to implement the things you've learned about your family and see how it turns out.

I can already tell you that people like attention, so these people that you are trying to change will first see that you have them in mind. Now, you don't want to rush into anything. Just keep your eyes open and your ears listening.

Your Friend,

John

Working Hard

On Thursday John was thinking about his subjects and decided that he'd better get this new book started. He figured that now that he was getting to know his subjects, he knew how to start his new book. John was reading the information that he had gathered from the blog and started out with writing short stories about each character that grew as the writing turned to fiction.

By Friday John had finished two chapters and was amazed at himself. John was reading and editing these two chapters and stopped because he didn't like how fictitious it was getting.

Friday night snuck up on John, and as he logged on to the blog, he found that all four subjects of the work group had logged on. They all were chatting about their week. John let them as he skimmed through the posts that were long.

Bill4267: I was at the family group on Wednesday to give my advice on the experiences I've had with my wives. John asked me to write about my past relationships, what worked and what didn't work. I think he wanted me to see how they were different people. I found the type of girl that I want and the type of girl that is good for me.

Sally1974: That is good. So are you looking for what you want or what is good for you?

Bill4267: I think I have friends and family to fill my jar, so I'm looking for what I want.

Jill1959: Fill your jar?

Bill4267: Yeah, John sent me an e-mail after that meeting saying that I should take what Amy said to me in stride, and he thought that what I told her was good for her relationship with her husband. He added a story to all of the e-mails: "Jar of Life." I'm sure he will add it to tonight's e-mails.

Timmy1982: I've been writing about my week at work and I have seen more than usual. I mean, I've became more observant.

Jill1959: That's the idea about writing a journal.

Timmy1982: Right, but even throughout the day I see more and I want to write it in my journal. My post is just the highlights of my week, but you should read my journal. No, don't ask, but it's like I'm seeing more or I understand more.

Jill1959: That's good. That is how I feel I'm helping out some of my coworkers. I'm just more observant.

Bill4267: That is what John is trying to get us to see.

John2010: Bill is right, I am helping you to see what makes your world tick. After you see that, you can change the small things in your life to cause big changes.

Sally1974: Like at work the other day, I just had to make a small effort to change how one of my bosses saw me. I just needed to speak up, which sounds easy but not for me. I listened and added comments where I knew the answer and then some guy asked me how it was done and I spoke up.

Bill4267: I read that in your post and that got me thinking that you should look back at encounters like that. When they have had positive outcomes and when your coworkers just ignored what you had to say.

Sally1974: Well, I think it's because I'm acting more positive and less ditsy. I used to be unsure of myself with everything and I would shake it off with a stupid comment. Now when I'm more observant I can see that people don't look to me for answers. I have proven to some of them that I really do know what I'm doing.

Jill1959: That's good. Now that I'm more thought of as a cat and less than just as a sheep, people look at me differently. I mean, at work people are showing me the respect that I was looking for and at lunch the girls are talking to me and not just around me, if you know what I mean.

Timmy1982: Yeah, I know what that's like. At the lounge at work, guys are always doing that. I mean, they sometimes even talk about me when I'm right there. I mean, this used to happen, but at that seminar that I went to and helped out with the after party I met those guys that were doing that. They still belittled me a bit, but I think they do that to look bigger themselves. I was listening to the different groups at this after party, and I started talking with a part of the table from my floor.

Bill4267: I read that and it sounds like you made friends, but I'm not too sure about how you said that half of them think you're a clown now.

Timmy1982: Yeah, I can't believe I did that. I knew I was going to be put onstage, but I didn't mean to say all that.

John2010: That's right, when you put someone in the spotlight, they say more than they would in the shadows. Now, Timmy, you were actually in the spotlight and talking jokes, but I am saying to give someone more attention to get more out of them.

Sally1974: Yeah, that was funny, Timmy. John, I know what you're saying, but that is sometimes too much work. After work some of the girls always go out and I was talking with the one that I work with as her friends asked if she was coming and she asked me to join. I was talking to her at that time to see if I could go out with these girls and make the connections that I need. This girl can be so exhausting, though.

Jill1959: I thought that was funny how you asked one of the other girls to relieve you when she got back from the bathroom.

Sally1974: That was a good call too, because they all laughed and the others started talking to me and asking my advice. I never had that happen, but now with my newfound confidence I can advise others. I know how that sounds, but really it feels good.

John2010: That's all we are trying to do. Make our lives feel better.

Bill4267: Yes, and get ahead at work. I'm using this theory of talking more and the connections I've made got to my boss and he's taking a different look at me. That has me worried about what he'll see, but that is my problem that I can handle. What I'm happy about is that I got his attention.

Jill1959: That's great. Now my boss is looking at me with different eyes, but that's all I want, is to get them to think of me as a can do and less as whatever.

Bill4267: Jill, don't you want a promotion at work?

Jill1959: Well, a raise would be nice, but I am happy with my job.

Sally1974: I would love a raise and a manager's posting, because then I could delegate my work easier. It wouldn't feel like someone was doing me a favor that I would have to pay back, because I would be a manager or a junior manager.

Timmy1982: Right. Well, I am happy with my position, but I want to be recognized more for my work. If I was more assertive and bold, I think that would go a long way in being appreciated for my work. I hope after they see how hard I'm working, they give me a raise.

John2010: I hope you all are finding the people that you should change to make the most of your efforts.

Jill1959: I have found that if I change how I act or respond to some people, I gain the respect that I'm looking for from everyone.

John2010: Right, but who are these people and why do they have such an affect? Ask yourself that and find how to affect their sands. Oh, I didn't tell you all about the sands of your life yet, did I?

Sally1974: Bill told us something about that. Golf balls fill our lives, but sand changes it or something.

John2010: I'll add the story to the e-mail I'll be sending you all. I have skimmed through your posts and it looks like you have found the people who affect your work life the most. Now you need to find the small things that affect their lives, so you can shape them into what you want.

Jill1959: I don't know that I want to change people's shape of life.

John2010: Jill, you will be surprised how useful and easy it is if you know how to cause your boss to have you do things that you enjoy doing. Work is just one place where you can use this skill. If you get good at looking for these things in every part of your life, your life will change for the better.

Bill4267: I was reading your post Timmy. John is having us write notes of our days for a good reason. It's so that we can get a better look at our days. I have written a few pages of past relationships and I'm seeing how to create the relationships that I want at work, at home, and with friends.

John2010: Try to write these notes in the third person. You'll be telling yourself, "I should have done this or that." Now, trust me, it will help to see yourself in a third person's view, that is what this group is for, and it will help you to keep active in your own life.

Sally1974: I know how hard it is. I've just been acting half as confident as I should, but I have acted better.

Timmy1982: With most people it is. I have had a hard time, but I push myself into acting...really just so I have something good to put into my post.

Sally1974: Last weekend was great, but I couldn't do that.

Timmy1982: Well, I kind of fell into that, or was it pushed?

Jill1959: I found out by accident that if I just speak up to the right people, it can cause big change.

John2010: That is the best way to do it. "You just have to Follow Through." Thanks, I think that's all for tonight.

John logged off feeling proud, but then he checked himself as he always did. *Now, are these subjects of mine grasping the concept fully?*

As John reads the posts in detail, he raised his eyebrows at spots and smiled during others. John finished with a shake of his head as he wrote some detailed suggestions on how to find the sands of life. John did thank Bill for telling the others how helpful it is to review your own life. At the bottom of each e-mail, John added the story of the Jar of Life.

> *Dear Friends,*
> *I am happy that most of you have grasped this theory, but it doesn't look like you have found the sands that you should change to affect the people that you want to change. You need to look closely at these people's lives to find the sands in their lives…*
> *Your Friend,*
> *John*

Finding Friends

John went to the park for lunch and watched the people around him interacting with each other as he ate his hoagie. John's eyes wandered and were drawn to the walking path to the women in tight shorts. Two women walking by were gabbing about a friend that has had a loss. These two women were trying not to have to deal with this girl. John just had to listen until they had past.

A man and a woman by the bench not far from where John was seated started to raise their voices at each other. John couldn't help hearing every last word, and as the woman stormed off, he looked up and almost reached out, but just sat up straight. The man was shaking his head and looking at the ground in front of him. John almost reached out to this man. *Didn't you hear...? You should have said...* John just finished his hoagie and left.

Monday came around and John wrote more pages about his subjects from the blog. He wasn't happy with how it was turning out. He had trouble figuring out how to write half the story, and was trying to write one complete story about eleven strangers.

The hour drew near, so John got a soda and logged on to the site. He found that Bill has logged in to the friends group today. John looked over the posts and found one from Bill that talked about how he had reviewed his experiences with his friends.

Bill4267: Mike. I have read today's post and it looks like some of your new friends aren't very good friends. I haven't been to these meetings, but it does look like you have found a subgroup of friends that you like.

Mike1991: Yes, and I may have been a bit harsh about Jay, but he does get on my nerves. The other friends say that's how he is. I told Brad about it and that just made it worse, but Jay stopped it for a bit.

Tarry1978: Bill, I have looked at my past relationships also, but writing details about my day every night is enough writing for me. I am more creative, so I like looking at the big picture, not the specific details.

John2010: That is good, be creative. Create a scrapbook of images, things, and words about your relationships. A scrapbook is a good idea for all of you. It will help your creative thinking process. Creative thinking is how you find new ways to confront old problems. You all should be looking at people differently now. Your friends should look like different people now that you are looking deeper inside their shells.

Anna1983: Yeah, that Glass Jar you told us about helps me look at my own life and put into perspective some things. Alex has in his post how he used the glass jar to categorize his friends. I was starting to look at it that way and made a jar for each subgroup and then I made jars for each person.

Alex1986: I named my jars and then I named the different groups of jars.

John2010: That is good, you're taking apart your life and taking the time to look at it. Now, don't get overwhelmed, Tarry. You can use a scrapbook of images to help you see your life. Just an idea for anyone to do, but you can make a collage of images or words that represent a person or group. You can use the collages to categorize these relationships by importance.

Tarry1978: John, I am having trouble finding my sands.

John2010: Well, Tarry, you may see your sands in bunches. Make a collage of one of your friends, and the pieces of the collage are your sands. If the collage of your friend is missing a piece, then your friend would be something different. Remember to make this collage from a third-person perspective.

Mike1991: Yeah, I'm having trouble with that, but I think I do know what you mean. I made a list of my friends and then I made lists about my friend's, friends. At first I started these lists about how I saw them, but then I asked myself, "What does Stacy and Rachel think of Nancy?" and then, "How do Rick and Scot see her?" Yeah, that gave me three lists about one of my friends.

Bill4267: That's a good way to think about it, but how do you know how Stacy or Rachel think.

Anna1983: Nancy is that new girl in this week's post. She seems nice, but I don't know these other people.

John2010: Stop. You aren't supposed to know these people. Mike and each of you should get to know your own friends. This group is not to socialize. It's to help each other learn about our friends and help us change our lives for the better.

Anna1983: Right, right, I just like relating names to these characters. I know this is anonymous group help. I guess if Mike wants us to know them, then he'll let us know.

Mike1991: I haven't told you all about them because they weren't really a part of my life.

Tarry1978: Right. Well, I'm not too sure that I want to tell you all about Jamie's new friends. I am finding that some of them are more important to her than I thought. Jamie is important to me and I don't want to lose her to them, so I am taking a better look at each of them.

Bill4267: That's what we all should do, but the hard part is to see them how others do. I mean I have asked friends about people at work to get there thoughts. One friend from work started to ask why I was…

John2010: Mike and all of you, the person you pass on the street every day is a part of your life, but it's how much you allow that person to influence your life that matters. If you say hi and throw a smile and receive one in return, then that does affect you in some way. These things are the dust in the sands that don't actually matter, but how much dust does it take to make a grain of sand?

Bill4267: Wow, that is deep, I have found dust in my life that I thought of calling sand. I thought again and told myself that it doesn't matter what happens to that dust.

John2010: If it matters to you, then it matters. I am running with this, because I want you to see that every little thing can affect your life and the lives of the people you are trying to change.

Alex1986: My jars have gotten many. I know I just have one jar, but I need jars for the golf balls in my jar. I need to fill the jars of my golf balls with what makes them and then fill the jars of my marbles.

Tarry1978: I think I am seeing more of the sands in my life, but filling a jar with other people's lives seems too much. I can see it, but I think I'll make a collage of their life; it sounds like a good idea.

Bill4267: I have been making lists, but yeah, fill these people's jars with what makes them what they are to me. Or to the third person. That is how other people see you or your friends, but isn't it more important how you see them?

John2010: Well, I'm trying to get you all to see your friends for what they really are, so you can see their agenda of life. How are they using you to make their lives what they are, so you can change them to fit your agenda of life?

Anna1983: Agenda of life sounds shrewd, but I can see it. It's what I want for my life, and you're helping us see how to get it.

Mike1991: I think I need to find my agenda for life.

John2010: This idea of finding what makes your life with the jar or just a list or even a collage will help you find what is important in your life. You want to use this list to find who to change in your life and then make a list for them that has more of a third-person view. Mike, if you like Nancy, then who do you change in your group of friends so that they all accept her?

Mike1991: I do like her. We laughed a lot when we worked together in that class. I guess I should try to get the head of the big group to accept her or a head of a subgroup. I think she is on a different spectrum from those friends though.

Alex1986: Mike, do you like her friends? Maybe you should leave those other so-called friends.

Mike1991: I have connected with a few of these friends, and really I wouldn't have if I wasn't in this group.

John2010: Alex, I'm sure you have good intentions, but we need to help Mike to see who he wants as friends.

Tarry1978: I'm trying to get Jamie to see that her new friends aren't good for her. I'm seeing that not all of these friends of hers are bad; they are just different.

Anna1983: That was so funny how you tried to tell her that she was just looking for something different. You need to show her in a more indirect way, but I can also see how you like being direct about things you care about.

Tarry1978: I care about Jamie too much to let her change and have her leave me. What I need is to find what her new friends' agendas are and make her see that they aren't hers.

Bill4267: That's right, you need to make a collage of this new group and then find its structure. Then you can see how to shape its structure in a way that Jamie won't like.

Anna1983: That sounds too devious.

Mike1991: Yes, but if you want to cause change, you always hurt the people who don't want to change. I've seen that and I don't like it, but I think that is why I was stuck for so long.

Alex1986: Right, I've had friends that just left the group I was in when it changed, but then some of the groups of friends I've had weren't that tightly knit.

Tarry1978: So what you are saying is that I need to do what I am finding is hard for me to do. I'll try using these other ways of finding what makes these annoying people tick. Then I need to find a way to get Jaime to see it or change them to what Jaime won't like.

John2010: Alex, your post was short today. Did you have a fall-out or something?

Alex1986: I just had a lot of work this week. Oh, and my girl's not talking to me.

Anna1983: Need any help with that?

Alex1986: NO!

John2010: Okay, let's end tonight with that. I hope you all see how the little things in your life can make a big difference. It just takes a little thing to change other people's lives. You just need to find it.

John logged off, but he thought some of this group stayed on to try to get Alex to talk about his girlfriend. He did copy all of the posts and read them thoroughly so that he could give the best advice to each of his subjects. Now John thought that this group got his idea, but he still didn't think they all were using it to get all they wanted.

Dear Friends,

I hope you all are using these skills to their fullest. I believe that you all can see how the little things affect our lives. I don't know how to emphasize it any more that it is important to find these things in your closest friends. All of you think you know them, but until you have taken this closer look, you can't say that you do.

Your Friend,

John

Join the Family

John took it easy on Tuesday thinking and writing about his new friends. He kept having to remind himself that they were just subjects for his new book. He enjoyed imagining the lives of these subjects a bit too much and told himself, "These people are stupid. Can't they see? Just that one thing will…"

That was just one way John kept his life above everybody else's. Wednesday night came around and John logged on to the blog page with Bill and Amy already complaining. John skimmed though the posts and joined Amy and Bill as Sledge and Rick logged on.

Bill4267: My second wife kept her life to herself mostly. I think that's why it lasted so long.

Amy1979: I want to share my life with my husband, and I want him to share his life with me.

John2010: Amy, I read that you are letting him tell his story more. Bill, I'm glad that you have joined us, but you aren't here to argue, just to tell and listen.

Bill4267: Right. I'll read the new posts and see how I may contribute to this blog.

As they all read the newly posted posts, John just skimmed through them and typed his first reactions.

John2010: It looks like you all are making good progress with little effort. That is my theory, that if you change specific but small things in your world it can have a big effect on your life. Amy, I see that you have started a hobby that your husband asked you about. You two had a conversation that he started that you led to much more. Sledge, I think your stepfather would be a good role model to follow and watch how he treats strangers. You can find out a lot about your wife's family by spending time with Andy also. Rick, I'm glad to hear that you are becoming friends with some of your wife's coworkers. I can see that you are finding good info on your wife, but you didn't write how you are using that info.

Rick1982: I have been listening to Crista's stories until my mind wanders away. I want to get straight to the point with her, but I don't want Crista to pull away from me into her own world. Some of the people I've talked to tell me she has been drifting away at work more recently when Crista feels confronted with more things. I've seen her drift away at home, but I thought that just happened because she's bored.

Amy1979: Rick, you have told us that she works at a big store and she has recently been given more responsibilities. I'm thinking that it's good that you don't confront her at home and it's good that you are listening to how her days are going. I think what you need is to ask more questions so that you don't lose interest in her story and be more engaged with the story of her day.

John2010: I agree, and you do need to make her feel like she can share with you and that you enjoy it. Laugh at the least funny things, but don't overdo it with the things you think are actually funny. If you want to be more engaged with your wife, then you need to make it fun for her to talk with you. It will grow into more than you want.

Bill4267: That is funny, John, when I've tried to save one of my marriages by talking and acting like I enjoyed it. Well, it's never good acting like something you're not.

John2010: Right, but if you can gain more out of it than you might lose, then it's okay, but Bill is right that you might not want to show something you're not, too often.

Bill4267: That's because she might start to expect it.

Amy1979: You need to fake it a bit in any relationship if just a little.

Bill4267: Okay, but I didn't want to always be on edge with my wives. Or, one of them wanted to know my daily agenda and when I lied I had to keep that lie going. It was good at the beginning, but one mistake and she tracked me down.

John2010: Don't interrogate your loved ones, just listen to their stories better and let them tell it. Listen closer and you'll hear more than they mean to say. By doing this you can learn to lead them into telling you what you want to know. Faking it isn't lying; it's just how you present yourself to the quest.

Rick1982: I'm not that good at holding a conversation, so I don't know how to bend my words like that.

Amy1979: My husband isn't good at carrying a conversation either, so I usually have to lead the conversation. Recently

I've been listening to his story more and he tells more. I just need to ask small questions that lead to more, but he actually gets tired of talking. When I notice this I start telling him about my day.

John2010: Yes, that's how it works. Listening more and talking more often can bring you closer, but you are listening for the small things. If you learn how to change these things that affect this person, you'll know how to have the affects you want upon this person to make the changes you want.

Bill4267: Okay, I think I get it, and looking in hindsight, I can see what I could have done with my wives to make some of the changes I wanted. I should take a look at those relationships.

John2010: Write it down. Make a folder of past relationships that worked, and one for those that didn't work. You will find out why they worked or didn't and use that knowledge to form the relationship you want. Now, Sledge, I see that you have spent time with your brother-in-law and father-in-law. It looks like you found that your brother-in-law acts differently with his father.

Sledge1984: Yeah, Andy's father controls him. I mean, it is scary how his father even controls strangers.

Bill4267: I used to have a friend that did that. He told me that he was just good at reading people and guessing their responses. His girlfriend hated it. I think that's why she dumped him.

John2010: Bill, are you still friends with him?

Bill4267: No, he was a boyfriend of one of my second wives' friends.

John2010: If any of you know someone who knows this stuff, watch them closely as they pay attention to the person that is getting the attention. You can learn a lot just from paying more attention to the right people.

Amy1979: You mean like you.

John2010: If you find anyone like me, it's best to look the other way. I'm here trying to help you all see how to change your lives for the better. From your posts it seems that my ideas are helping you all find your way. Now we meet here each week to share our posts and gain a nonjudgmental third-eye view.

Sledge1984: Yeah, thanks. I'm not worried about Andy with my sister now. Now I'm worried about getting too close to him.

Amy1979: Sledge, Andy's not gay from what I read. Yes, you make him sound gay, but you aren't supposed to write these posts with your opinion leading our views.

Rick1982: Right, but it is funny how paranoid you get.

Sledge1984: What???

John2010: I'm glad it's not just me that sees that, but, Sledge, we aren't judging you. Your posts are supposed to be telling the facts of your week, not your story of your week.

Rick1982: Right, I know it's hard to separate yourself from your week, but that's how you see the truth of your week.

John2010: Bill, you were chatting with Amy before I got here and you pointed out that she likes to control her husband. How might she show him that he is in charge of his own life?

Bill4267: Well, let him be. I mean, give him freedom. I was reading her post and it sounds like she doesn't approve of his new friends. She says that she is letting him go out with them, but it still sounds like she is interrogating him upon his return.

Amy1979: I'm just asking how Jim's night out was. I try to let him tell the story, but he stops talking, so I ask questions.

Bill4267: Sara kept track of my every movement of the day. She would start out asking how was my day, and I'd tell her, but before I could get away she would ask what happened next.

John2010: Bill, I'm guessing she just was looking for more details, but, Amy, it's how you ask that makes all the difference. Don't ask Jim what happened next, as Bill pointed out, but ask about something he has told you. If you show interest in what Jim's telling you, it will lead him into telling more.

Rick1982: That's right, I was trying to listen to my wife more, so I was making comments about what she was talking about. She started to clarify what she was saying by telling me about another friend that was in the same situation.

Amy1979: Well, Jim isn't that forthcoming with his friends, or his life for that matter.

John2010: Amy, you are starting out good but you need to be more patient with Jim and let him learn to enjoy sharing things with you.

Bill4267: Right, I think that was the problem with Sara: she was draining. I think you need to learn to laugh with your husband about things in both of your lives with each other.

Rick1982: That's right, I have been talking and laughing more with my wife. It seems that makes her more open with me, or like John told us to listen closer you may hear more than is meant to be heard. I have written a note to Have Confidence and to Step Up. Crista saw it on top of our toilet and I told her it is just a reminder. So she wrote on it Remember, and every day she adds to the list of things to remember.

Sledge1984: Does it work?

Rick1982: Well, I have been remembering to stand out more at work and with my friends. The lists help too.

John2010: Great, you all should have a note. That is a good place for it too. You use the toilet before you go to bed, you use it when you wake up, you use it before going out, and you use it when you get home. Well, our time is up, so I'll be going, but remember to look deeper into the people you think you know.

John logged off and after backing up the blog entries, he reread the posts and wrote more detailed suggestions. In this e-mail John added something to look out for.

When you are talking with family you don't try too hard because you know them and they know you. The old "We all know why we're here, let's get on with it" syndrome. You don't feel you have to "sell" the idea to your family. This makes it less likely that you'll plan your presentation deliberately, but you should plan, and yes it should be a presentation, to get the idea across to them in more depth. Don't forget to plan to listen to what even your family has to say.

Dear Friends,

I'm glad to hear that most of you are making good process in using my theory of changing your life. The thing's that I've listed are just to keep your eye's opened. Now that you are learning to listen better, you will find who you should be listening to and you are learning to read people better.

Your Friend,

John

Friendly Work

On Thursday, John reviewed the work group's posts and saw how they'd changed. He thought he saw how they had used what they'd learned in this group, but he kept reminding himself that he just saw what he wanted to see. John was a realist who tried to see the truth, but sometimes he saw the truth and let it pass. He tried too hard not to see a truth that he was looking for, because he knew that even he had preconceptions.

John knew that the worst thing was that he couldn't see everything in every way, so he had to stop himself from trying. He had learned to accept things for what they were, but he changed what he could into what he wanted. John had been reading about using emotions intelligently. Friday night arrived quickly, so John logged on to the site early and found Bill and Jill chatting about their jars.

Bill4267: I have been building jars about people at work and seeing their relationships better. Some of the relationships between people at work are strained by the work they do with each other. I even see them eating lunch together, but I see that they aren't really together. I thought about what John said about starting clubs or groups with like-minded people.

Jill1959: That's right, the girls that I have started to talk with about my antique doll collection wanted to come with me to a show and sale this weekend.

Bill4267: I read your post and it's great to see that you have found some people that respect you and like you. That may not have come out right, but I see that you are doing better at work with your coworkers.

Jill1959: I have been making lists about everyone and how they relate with each other. Those lists have opened my eyes and I have found who I need to get closer to at work to get the jobs I want.

John2010: I read your post and that is what these jars help you find.

Jill1959: Oh, I just make lists and categorize them by most important things I want to change.

John2010: That's right, the jars of life are just metaphors, and the lists you make take apart the jars of each of your coworkers. I skimmed Sally's and Timmy's posts and it looks like they have been building good jars also. I was thinking of introducing you all to how you use emotions at work to gain the upper hand while you finish reading the posts.

John2010: Emotional intelligence is important at work, because most of the time you are working with coworkers. Now, you can find information on-line about interacting at work, but there are a few things that I'd like to point out. Working in a group or team of coworkers, you should never blame someone for a problem. Say, "We have a problem. How are we going to fix this?" Use *we* so that the entire group takes part in the solution. If it is your fault, then take credit first: "I messed up. How are we going to fix this?"

John2010: When you are selling something, a product, a service, or an idea, you should use *empathy*. If you have trouble relating with someone, then you can fake it, by using a story that relates to what they're feeling. Empathy is identifying with and understanding another's situation, feelings, motives, or the attributions of their feelings to an object.

John2010: I stressed these last two things because they make it easier for others to enjoy your company. If people enjoy being in your company, then you will find that opportunities will come much easier.

Jill1959: John, I am very empathetic, sometimes too empathetic for my own good.

John2010: Yes, that can be a problem, but if you can detach yourself from a situation, that can be invaluable. When you are in a bad place, you put your mind in a good memory. As in when you have lost something, the fastest way to get over it is to replace it. If you have or can create a good memory that you can hold on to? You can use it when you are feeling bad—just bring that memory back to the front of your mind.

Sally1974: I have memories of being at the beach that always cheer me up.

John2010: Even better! A location of a happy memory is something that can take you away from that bad place and feeling you have. Just close your eyes and tell yourself, "I'm at the beach!"

Timmy1982: I like that, and when you say if you can't relate, fake it. I hate people who can't accept blame for a mistake.

If you say, "We have a problem," that person will know it's their fault, but they don't have to be on point to fix it.

Jill1959: Oh, I hate being blamed for a problem. When I know it's my fault I just clam up. I can see how saying, "My bad, how can we fix it?" is good, because it makes the others laugh inside. I like people that can laugh at themselves, but I am too embarrassed.

John2010: Jill, when you feel embarrassed go to the beach and smile.

Bill4267: I have learned not to be embarrassed about anything, but I can't laugh at myself. I've laughed at a situation that I get myself into after the fact. I have learned to be courteous for other people situations, but is that empathy?

John2010: Yes, Bill, and common courtesy is important to use with everyone, because people will remember you for it. Now, I know that you have ideas of who you need to affect to get ahead at work. These things I mention are not just to be used with them, because if these people see you acting differently with other people, they may ask why, and transparency is important, because people don't like being deceived.

Bill4267: Transparency is when you don't lie, and, well, I try not to lie. Isn't this idea we are trying to use just a way to get away with lying?

Jill1959: I was concerned with that last week, because I don't like lying. I came to the conclusion that we are learning to read people to affect them in ways that benefit our lives.

Timmy1982: You two are funny! We deceive people every day, or at least I do. I just let the people that I am the closest to really know me. I wear that mask every day that we all wear for the public. We have to be Politically Correct with strangers.

John2010: That's right, Timmy, we all wear masks. We wear masks with our closest friends because we don't want to lose them. Don't be concerned with lies. If you use this right, then the fabrications that we create will just be noticed by you.

Sally1974: Now, I'm okay with lying, but I never thought this was lying. I just thought John was teaching us how to read people better. To look at ourselves and our lives from the third-person perspective to make our lives better.

John2010: Exactly!

Jill1959: Okay! I guess that is all right. Now we should use what we have learned from these lists to make the right decisions on how we treat people.

Bill4267: Right, but I treat people right. It's just what I say isn't always right.

John2010: From your posts it sounds like most of you treat people with respect. You should use common courtesy with everybody at work to make them want to work with you. I think I should mention this, "When you do something right, your whole team did it."

Timmy1982: That's right. This manager I've been trying to get closer to does that. He never takes credit for his good work, he gives the hole team credit. The group of men I've been using to get closer to this manager have trouble with sharing the blame.

Bill4267: Yeah, when something goes wrong at work, it's the other guy's fault. I wouldn't want to be blamed for losing a contract that is worth millions.

Timmy1982: Right, because if I get blamed for losing money, then I won't get that raise I'm looking for.

Bill4267: Yeah, you'll get fired!

John2010: Haven't you heard the story about a college football player that won the Heisman? He did not win it because he won the Big Ten Championship game, but because he told the truth and lost it.

Jill1959: Oh my God, I've heard stories like that, but they're fiction. No one, or at least I, couldn't take responsibility for something like that.

Bill4267: Oh, it's been done, but just by great men that have already made themselves.

Sally1974: The greatest people are remembered for their failures, but they are still great. Like Hillary Clinton is a great secretary of state, but will be remembered for letting her husband cheat on her with Monica.

Timmy1982: What there wasn't any great Clintons in history 8)).

Bill4267: I remember Monica.

Jill1959: Yeah, I remember her too, but I don't remember Hillary being great.

John2010: People, that's neither here nor there. Now, we haven't talked about tonight's posts, but I can see that you all understand how looking deeper into someone's life makes you see them differently. I want you to find ways to use what you've learned about these people. Be aware that people remember the little things, as in an extra effort to be courteous, and when you share the success, you want to be as transparent as possible.

John logged off after that to let them chat, but again he rereads the posts and was feeling proud of himself. He could see with no doubt that this group was understanding his idea and working with it. John read that Jill and Sally were gaining the respect that they were looking for, and Timmy and Bill were making good connections.

In this e-mail John asked them to use the three principles that he pointed out in tonight's blog and gave them a helpful list of things to keep in mind:

People like people who . . .	People dislike people who . . .
• Pay attention to their opinions And their ideas • Talk to them on their level • Show them respect • Tell them the truth • Make an effort to connect with them • Have a sense of humor	• Are disingenuous and manipulative • Can't see past their own noses • Pretend to be something they are not • "One-up" and always shift the conversation back to themselves • Use candor at the expense of others • Are overly serious about everything

Treatment of Friends

John did some research about the different masks people use with their friends and why people use them. Over the weekend he had gone out to Central Park for lunch and to watch how friends react with each other. John found that the easiest types of friends to find and categorize were social friends and true friends.

This Saturday, John had started to take apart groups of social friend networks. He was thinking of how Mike had taken apart his network of friends at school. John noted a large group of friends in their early twenties were gathering for a picnic in the park. At first glance he noted how people joined this party of friends in subgroups. Most of these subgroups moved within this party of friends together.

As John was looking a bit too closely, a young woman left her subgroup and went over to a large man from this party of friends, but not from her subgroup. John was interested. *I wonder what their relationship is. Or is she from his subgroup and is visiting others?*

John was looking at this young woman who was just talking to this one man, and saw him leave her standing there with a look of despondency. Then he noticed where this large man was off to. John sat up, took his last bite, and stood up as this man approached him.

Sunday afternoon, Jon did go to Central Park again to watching different groups of friends, observing from a distance. He did talk himself out of getting a beating the other day, but he kept his eyes moving today.

Monday came and John went through his routine. As he reviewed the friends group's posts, he noted the different types of friendships. He could see that most of the subjects did find the jars of their friends. Now John felt that he needed to make sure they knew how to use them.

John logged on to the blog page to find that all four of the subjects were there with long posts that he just skimmed through. John found Alex trying to explain how to work with different groups of friends. Mike was having trouble with his new large group of friends accepting his new friends.

Alex1986: I once brought a friend from Germantown Academy to my beach house. I knew that this kid from school might have trouble loosening up, but he had trouble with my best beach bud. This kid was saying that my bud was too undomesticated for him, and he actually used "undomesticated." I just needed to show him how to see my bud how I saw him.

Mike1991: I don't think I want them to see Nancy how I see her.

Alex1986: No! How do you see her friends? Or do you expect her to change for your friends?

John2010: Now, if she changes, then she won't be what you love.

Tarry1978: I thought of that with Jaime, so I tried to see her new friends for what she sees in them. Mike I think you need to show this group of friends that are accepting you more what you see in Nancy and her friends. It just takes one of them to accept her to show the group. I've gotten to know one of Jaime's new friends, and now her other friends are getting to know me and vice versa.

Anna1983: Right, DON'T try to change Nancy.

John2010: Okay, people, I have found some information that will help you all to use what you've found out about these people you are trying to affect.

John copied and pasted the information from Friday's blog. They all took time to read the information as John posted Fridays replies. John shared the views that the work group had about using these skills. He started to explain how to communicate with different kinds of people and how to make the right connections.

John had to stop himself, and finished with:

John2010: Friends, I do tend to run on, but I'm trying to help you communicate with these friends that you want to change. Now, I try to keep it vague so that you can use what you think is relevant to your situation. I don't mean to be telling you what will work with your friends. You need to use those lists about your friends' lives to choose how you are to talk with them.

Anna1983: Great, I was reading this information thinking, "This guy is actually being useful," but now you tell us we have to find the way that we think we should go. Just kidding, I know that we have to do some work and find out how to make sure we are affecting our friends the right way.

Tarry1978: I think John just doesn't want us to come back saying, "It didn't work." He doesn't want to have to say, "That's not my fault."

Mike1991: I can see how this stuff should work. We just need to keep in mind who we are talking to and how to talk to them.

Alex1986: When you've had friends that are as different as my friends are, you need to change yourself before you think of changing them.

John2010: I couldn't have said it better myself. Now, I know you don't want to change anything big in your lives. That is why we are looking to change the little things or the sands in your lives and your friends' lives.

Tarry1978: What you told us last week was deep. How I made a collage of each of my friends. I started with the big things and kept piling on what made them who they are, and the pile got deep. I looked at the little things and as I took one or two away, I saw that it would change them. I don't want to change Jaime into something that I wouldn't like. Oh, and I looked closer at her new friends and I think I've found ways to change them.

John2010: Be careful, you don't want Jamie to find out that you are behind these changes in her new friends. She may not want you to hang with her and her new friends. The best way to start may be to befriend one of these new friends that isn't too close with the one you are trying to change.

Alex1986: One time at the beach I started to hang with a guy that got a new Jet Ski. When one of my close buds saw that I was hanging with him, he stopped hanging with me as much. I asked him, "What's going on?" and he just said, "I never liked that clown." So I stopped having as much fun on the Jet Ski, and I hung out with my bud more.

Tarry1978: Okay, right, I have to be sure that Jamie likes this other friend before I befriend them. Well, the girl that I don't like is more or less the leader of the subgroup that Julie has been getting together with.

Anna1983: Oh well, you should be careful. Like Alex has pointed out, you may alienate the wrong people. I wouldn't go about this in that way. I would probably be doing the wrong thing, but I would make this girl that you don't like Jamie being around mad at me. Or, ah, just not like being around me.

John2010: That may work if Jamie chooses you, but find out what attracted Jamie to this new group of friends and change that. Use the collages that you made to find out how she has changed. It has to be more than just that they are different. You should look at how they act together, or how the relationship they have, with Julie is different than your relationship.

Mike1991: I was thinking about who I could get to see that Nancy is cool, and they are a small subgroup of three that I was thinking to join. Is it okay to change subgroups?

John2010: It is early in this relationship with this group and it looks like you've been mostly with the top subgroup of this group. Yes, you have started to separate with Brad, but he is still part of that subgroup, so it is fine to find a more compatible subgroup.

Alex1986: Mike, don't be a window shopper! You should find a subgroup to settle down with soon. When I'm at the beach I know that these barneys won't be there next year, but there are some locals there every year who I stay tight with.

Anna1983: Mike, don't stick with that subgroup just because they are the head of the group. You need to be comfortable with them and they should be comfortable with you and what you have to offer.

Tarry1978: Great, that's the Saturday afternoon special. What they all are saying is right, but you should use these lists that John had us make to find the right people to get what you want. If this group isn't exactly what you want, then use the little things in these relationships to change it.

John2010: That's what I'm saying.

Mike1991: Yeah, I have, and I see what to do, but I think it is going to be harder than you're letting on, John.

John2010: You have done it already. Now you just need to keep at it. Your posts are showing us all how to cause change. I've looked at Alex's post and it doesn't show much, but it sounds like you know what I'm getting at.

Alex1986: I've been making lists and taking them apart about my girlfriend and her friends and family. I'm still trying to see the full picture. I have found some of the little things to affect her friends. I think I can use these friends to affect her family, but I'm not too sure if it will turn out good.

Anna1983: Alex, in your post you say that you want her family to like you as they like her friends. If you are thinking of making her family not like them by changing them? Well, I wouldn't do that. I would want these friends to like me and in return her family would like me better.

Alex1986: Right, but I used to go out with one of these friends and Jessie doesn't like us getting too close. Her other friend always keeps her distance from me.

Mike1991: I think she just doesn't want to become just one of the three friends that you date, and after that the friendship breaks up.

Alex1986: Well, I didn't really date Kim, but I see what you're thinking. I just screwed myself by screwing two friends.

Anna1983: Alex, are you the kind of guy that just has a friend of the opposite sex that is your girlfriend.

Tarry1978: Oh, I hate when guys are like that. Just because I'm talking to you doesn't mean I like you.

Alex1986: There are other girls that I'm friends with, but they are Jessie's friends.

John2010: Everything I have shared with you will help with making all kinds of friends. I would hope, if you are being friendly with one of your girlfriend's friends, that they should know that all you're looking for is to be friends. Alex, tell us more about Jessie's family in next week's post and see if you can find a connection to her brother or her father.

John logged off to let them chat about how womanizing Alex was by themselves. He reviewed all of their posts that were longer with more specific details. John was seeing how they were using his ideas, and he felt proud, but he saw how they could do better. He started writing his replies with details, but he tried to let them know that it was up to them how they used his ideas.

> *Dear Friends,*
>
> *I am happy to see that you are grasping the idea. We talked about how to use these lists and present ourselves to the people that we are trying to change. I hope that this information will help you all. Your posts are getting longer and with more important information. Now we need to write about more specific details in our posts and in our everyday notes.*
> *Your Friend,*
> *John*

Family Treatment

After sending the e-mails and inviting Alex to the family group, John went through his usual routine on Tuesday. By Wednesday night he was looking forward to seeing the progress that his subjects were making.

John logged in to the room and found that Alex and Sledge had been chatting about each other's problems. Alex updated the post from Monday and took a closer look at the relationships that Jessie's friends had with her family.

John2010: Alex, I'm glad you're here. I would like to share some information about how to talk to people and get the right message through to them. Alex, you read this on Monday, so take your time reading the others' posts.

John copied and pasted the same information about emotional intelligence with the responses from the other groups. He didn't want to have to repeat himself for today's subjects. John gave them all time to read the information and they were all satisfied with the responses John listed.

John2010: I think that if we focus on Alex tonight it will be helpful for us all.

Amy1979: I was reading his post and it sounds like he is having control issues. Not like mine, but I can see Jim in him. Alex isn't as timid as Jim, but at times Alex doesn't seem to take the needed actions.

Rick1982: I see that, but I think what he's saying is that he knows better. It's how he approaches Jessie that he may need help with. John just listed ways to get around situations.

Alex1986: I know, that was why I added that info to my post. About how Jessie acts when her friend is there. I don't touch some subjects when Kim is around.

Sledge1984: I wouldn't either. I think Amy just wishes Jim would talk to her about those things.

Amy1979: You just need to start talking to her about something she likes to make her comfortable. When you change the subject, try not to let her know it's you who is changing it. I think Jim just rolled his eyes and took a breath when I tried to do that once.

John2010: You want to sell the idea to her by talking about something you both enjoy and relate it to the subject that you are trying to talk about.

Rick1982: Yeah, I got Krista gushing about something before I started introducing the topic I wanted to talk to her about. I told you all about it in my post and I felt we really accomplished something there.

Sledge1984: Alex, what is up with her two best friends? It sounds like they are trying to keep their distance.

Alex1986: Well, they are, for two different reasons. I had a relationship with one, and the other one doesn't want one, but I think she's attracted to me.

Amy1979: They are a lost love and a forbidden love. Too bad they are your girlfriend's best friends, but it almost looks like you envy them.

Alex1986: I guess I envy the relationship that they have with Jessie's parents. I am trying to make it more comfortable to talk with Jessie's parents. These two friends talk with her parents fine, because those three have been friends since childhood.

John2010: How can you make your relationship with her parents be more like the relationship you have with her and her friends?

Alex1986: I've made a tree in MS Access taking apart Jessie's life. Her friends, her family, work relations, and acquaintances. I have also started to categorize the activities she does by how she likes to do them. I know that I should take a look at our relationship from the outside, but I'm having a hard time. As I make the trees I have to ask myself if my opinion is influencing my views.

Rick1982: Right. Well, we take our opinion out of the picture by thinking of these people as characters. At least that works for me. When I started my lists I had an image that I thought I was looking for. Then I looked through a window as if I didn't know what was on the other side. That took me away from the picture I wanted.

Alex1986: I can do something like that. Now I am trying to see how to avoid conflicts with Jessie and Kim. Conflicts have become a part of our relationship. I just don't want them to end the relationship.

John2010: Okay, that was what I wanted to bring to these meetings somehow. How to prevent conflicts and how to win them by collaboration. We all know confrontations aren't good for a relationship. I have told you about how to sell your idea and making the person think it's his/hers.

Amy1979: Yeah, like using emotional intelligence and empathy to affect how the person you are with sees things your way.

John2010: Right, but you want to see the conflict developing and take action to prevent it. There is a conflict that I can see developing with at least two of you here. *Equality* is a good way to prevent a building conflict. If one person is taking too much control of a relationship, that can build unwanted conflict. That is why *empathy* is a good way to gain control, but you want to show *equality* in your relationship.

Sledge1984: My wife has a lot of control, but I try to control her more like John has told Amy to do with Jim.

John2010: Who has the control in Alex's relationship with Jessie?

Amy1979: Jessie!

Rick1982: Kim!

John2010: I see, but the relationship is between Jessie and Alex. How Alex has shown that he knows what makes Jessie uptight and how he used that awareness to stop a conflict— that shows control. The use of collaboration is a way to gain control. Yes, with a collaborative relationship, there has to be some give-and-take. The best leaders use a collaboration to gain control and prevent conflict.

Sledge1984: Okay, so Amy should use more collaboration with Jim before he blows up at her.

Rick1982: That's being blunt. It looks like Jim isn't one to take action. In Amy's post it looks like she is trying to push him into making a decision, and John had to hold back from telling her not to do that.

John2010: Thank you, Rick, but please don't put words into my mouth or screen. Amy, don't take anything typed at any blog as it looks. You can't see the person's eyes, so you don't know if what is typed is just meant to be in jest. I do see trouble brewing, but so do you, I'm sure.

Amy1979: Yes, but Jim can be so frustrating at times. He just rolls his eyes a lot and he's doing it more now that I'm making more of an effort.

Sledge1984: That's because he sees that. He thinks you are acting different to get something.

Rick1982: You should listen to him more and be encouraging to hear more about what he wants to talk about. I can see that he would think you are just trying to get something by pushing him into saying what you want to hear.

Alex1986: Jessie does that to me. I have learned how to see when she doesn't want to hear me; she just wants me to tell her that she's right. I think everybody has times like that, but Jessie makes me feel like she is looking down on me.

John2010: That is one thing I wanted you to see. How you talk to someone can make a big difference. Now, Amy, how would you like Jim to talk?

Amy1979: Well, I wish Jim was more *assertive*. I know I should listen to what he wants to talk about, and seem interested, but I just want to get to the point.

John2010: Amy, try to use *equality* to gain Jim's trust and let him open up more to you. Alex, I think you should let Jessie know that you are her *equal* and don't let her look down on you as much. "Your words" I think Jessie likes having you on edge around her best friends, so talk to her about how these friends affect your relationship. Make her feel guilty first but don't push it.

Alex1986: How???

John2010: Put her on the defensive, then reassure her to make her feel as if she owes you, then bring up her friends and how they affect you. This hour goes by fast. Alex, you are always welcome here.

John signed off, leaving the group to their chatter. As he reviews the posts, he commented more on Rich's and Sledge's posts so they didn't feel neglected. John was happy to see that Sledge was talking with his wife's family more and was feeling more comfortable. He saw that Rick was finding that his wife was not happy with a friend at work. Rick was trying to make a better effort at home to let her express herself.

John added the posts about emotional intelligence to the e-mail and try to emphasize the use of collaboration.

Work Emotions

John had been researching how to talk with strangers at work. Most of what he found had to do with harassment at work. John hoped his subjects knew better than to look for sex at work, but he might mention it. John was thinking that the same thing applied with most relationships. If you make the other person think you are putting them ahead of yourself, it's hard for him not to like you.

John knew that if you give someone too much attention, they may get the idea that you like them more than you actually do. John just rolled his eyes. *That can cause problems. It's never what you intend it to be, it's what the people think you intended.*

Doing more research about not sending the wrong messages at work, John found a way to stop any misunderstandings. John intended to make that point to his subjects, and hoped Bill could help out with examples.

After John logged in to the blog room, he found Jill and Sally chatting about their posts. Jill had found a small group of women at work to share her hobby with. Sally was getting the respect that she was looking for at work.

Jill1959: When I was with the girls at a market show of collectables, we met other women that were into dolls more than the girls I brought. I even remembered to use the emotional intelligence there and I shared more at the show.

Sally1974: People are opening up more with me in the break room when I use emotional intelligence. Oh, and I am collaborating more with my coworkers, and I'm more opened with them. I'm trying to make them feel like they are more of a part of what I'm telling them about. I think how I would like to feel.

John2010: It looks like you two are using the emotional intelligence and it's changing your outlook at work. Now, I have done some research about work relations. I was thinking about misconceptions at work. Jill, I see that you just work with women and it looks like you are giving the right message, but, Sally, what has the reaction been from the men at your job?

Sally1974: Well, there is one man that I thought was coming on to me. When he asked me if I wanted some coffee after work, I just said, "I don't date coworkers…" He said, "No, no, I just wanted to get some coffee. I don't drink, but you can have some wine…" I stopped him. "No, really I have to go!" And he smiled and backed off quickly.

Bill4267: Yeah, he didn't want you to get the idea that coffee meant sex and report him. It's good to know that he doesn't drink.

John2010: Good, you caught that. Those things you should all be listening for. He didn't want to tell you that he doesn't drink, but he said it, and I hope you were paying attention. Sally, I don't know if you want to start a new relationship with this man, but you could start a conversation with him about coffee, wine, alcoholics, or anything on that topic. Now, I'm just using this coworker of Sally's as an example.

Jill1959: I have been listening and hearing things to use with my new friends at work. I used to not pay attention to half of what I heard from them, because I thought that they had no interest in me. I was prejudging them as they were prejudging me.

Sally1974: I am listening more at work, but the men I work with aren't that complex.

John2010: That man that asked you out. Don't prejudge him, you may want to take him up on getting a drink after work to make more connections. Now, don't dismiss him, just don't treat him any different at work than anyone else. If he sees that you are giving or getting this attention to all of your colleagues at his rank, then he won't get any ideas that he shouldn't.

Sally1974: I'm not in the army. We don't have ranks.

John2010: I mean importance to get your job done.

Bill4267: That's right, if you give extra attention to a guy at work who you aren't friends with, then who knows what he'll be thinking? I'm sure you know this, but equality is best to use at work with everyone.

Timmy1982: Right, I was working with a new team this week and I was putting them all first, and making sure I was incorporating everyone in the project. After we were finished, we went our separate ways to lunch. One of the women that was on the team saw me sitting alone eating my lunch and she came over.

Bill4267: Let me guess: you were giving her too much attention.

Timmy1982: I guess. She did say that she doesn't like eating alone. I almost said that I prefer it, but I thought she might take that the wrong way.

Sally1974: Didn't you want someone to eat with?

Timmy1982: No, I don't like to talk when I eat. Anyway, she was giving me a different view of the new team, because she has worked with most of them before. I have been working just with one guy most of my time at this agency. Right now he is working on a new project that didn't need me.

Jill1959: So, is this your first time to be team leader?

Timmy1982: I don't know that I'm much of a leader. I guess I am in charge of this project.

John2010: A team leader should make a point to show it.

Timmy1982: Right, I used the emotional communication that helped get the team moving in the right direction. Two of the team members are kind of at odds with how to go with their part of the project. I left them today saying that if they present their ideas by Monday, I would choose which one to use.

John2010: Be careful now. Two heads are better than one. On Monday I suggest that you be more assertive and get them working on the best presentation together.

Timmy1982: I was just going to use the idea that has the most done.

Bill4267: This is where emotions at work can just get in the way. You need to take charge and use the best idea for the project. Has that girl who you ate lunch with given you any insights on these two characters?

Timmy1982: Oh yeah, she says that these two guys are best friends and the one guy can be overdramatic and have fits. Her words. After I heard that, I was more attentive to how I communicated with him.

John2010: How did that make you feel? Having to work with someone who has an explosive personality. I was planning on bring up sending the wrong message and how to deal with explosive personalities. I think I explained that you shouldn't give one person extra attention, but someone with an explosive personality may need it.

Jill1959: There is a girl at work like that, but she is just overdramatic. She doesn't explode into violence, but she can have fits.

Bill4267: I have worked with guys that I could tell had to hold their punches.

John2010: I hope these guys know better than to get violent. To deal with an outburst, you need to understand what this person is trying to convey, but can't put into words. Timmy, I am guessing that these two guys are emotionally involved with their ideas. Try to let them know that you understand how they feel, and don't demean their idea. Get them to work on the one idea of your choosing by trying to incorporate how the other idea relates.

Jill1959: Yeah, at work one time two men were trying to convince each other that his plan was better, so the one guy pointed out how his plan was just like the other man's. They were totally different plans, but he was trying to show how they were the same.

John2010: Exactly! That is also called manipulation, but most people don't like to feel that they are being manipulated. You need to use emotional manipulation... I mean communication.

Sally1974: Right, you have told us to try to relate with the person's situation that we are trying to change. We should communicate to this person that we are just like them and can feel where they're coming from.

Bill4267: I had a coworker that I can see now was using emotional manipulation a lot, which I thought was annoying. I was out with a couple of coworkers after work and he was there. He was trying to bond with another guy there that was complaining about his in-laws. I just had to tell him to stop, it was just a joke.

John2010: Yes, being too emotional or using emotional communication with everyone can cause problems.

Sally1974: I thought we were supposed to treat everyone alike.

John2010: At work you don't want to overdo it with any one coworker. Your boss or head manager is a different story. Your coworker will see that you are acting different with them because of their higher position. Now, if you're out with a group of friends, you may not want to use emotional communication, because they joke with each other. If you are selling a product or an idea, that is when you use emotional manipulation. You are using it to get them to find a reason to buy the product or into the idea.

Jill1959: It can be draining to be emotional with everyone all day. I can see that we have to find the little things in life to see how emotional to be.

Timmy1982: I am using the little things about my coworkers and seeing how to change them just enough. I was thinking about what the girl said about those two guys, and at first it scared me, but now I think I see a way to attack the problem with those two. It shouldn't be that hard.

John2010: That is good, Timmy. Think positive. I have to go, but you guys can chat about how Timmy can choose the best idea without alienating the other guy's idea. But, Timmy, you need to choose the best plan for the job.

John logged off mainly because he felt that his subjects had the idea of using emotional communication when it was needed, and John hated repeating himself. He saved tonight's postings to the work group folder and just hit the pillow.

The next morning John woke early like usual, and after rereading the posts and writing the e-mails, he searched for more information to share. John didn't think the emotional manipulation was a good idea for the friends group. John read a story about how changing one little thing in somebody's morning can change their entire day. That was what his idea was about doing.

Finding the little things in people's lives that can make a big difference. John was first helping his subjects to read people better and deeper to find what made them who they were. Then he was helping them find the right way to change these people's lives or to change their own.

Reading Friendly Faces

Over the weekend, John read a story about reading emotions in faces. He went out and was observing people's expressions, just not too closely. John was finding himself wanting to know why some of these people were showing such feelings. He did check himself, because he knew better than to approach a stranger and ask, *Why are you feeling such things?*

On Monday John felt prepared to share how he translated the story he read and give advice on reading facial expressions.

Mike1991: Alex. Your advice was useful. I just wish I could read people better.

Alex1986: Well, the more time you spend with your new friends, the better you will learn to read them.

John2010: That's right, I was trying to find a shortcut to reading people's emotions. There's nothing like time and experience with someone to learn how you should read them. Longtime friends aren't the same people as they were years ago, so how do you read changes?

John2010: There are common facial expressions that are dead giveaways for how someone feels. Some common examples of feelings that can be expressed are:

• <u>Anger</u>	• <u>Fear</u>
• <u>Concentration</u>	• <u>Frustration</u>
• <u>Confusion</u>	• <u>Glare</u>
• <u>Contempt</u>	• <u>Happiness</u>
• <u>Desire</u>	• <u>Sadness</u>
• <u>Disgust</u>	• <u>Snarl</u>
• <u>Excitement</u>	• <u>Surprise</u>

John2010: Happy, Sad, Anger, and Confused may be the most obvious facial expressions. These other expressions may be less apparent, but they are there. I was trying to get you all to look at these people from what they have done and what they are doing. This is a good way to find how to use emotional communication with the people you know. If these people change or you find new people, what do you do? Facial expressions are a good way to find out how to use emotional communication .

Anna1983: I can read lips, but reading faces seems hard. I have tried it, but more than half the time I'm wrong.

Tarry1978: Oh, I have thought I knew how someone was feeling just by her eyes and I got into trouble.

John2010: Girls, calm down. Reading facial expressions is just to help shape your words. People get in trouble when they think they know the whole truth from a smile or a cringe. You need to know the context of what the expression is based upon. That is why I want to look at the four major facial expressions to help find a base for your friends' facial expressions.

Mike1991: Okay, I can connect most of these facial expressions to some of my new friends, but what is a snarl?

John2010: To snarl is to cringe your eyebrows with flaring nostrils… All mammals do it. Think of a dog growling. With humans it isn't always to show anger. It can show disgust, surprise, or anything in between.

Tarry1978: Oh yeah, I know girls that snarl a lot.

John2010: Well, how does she move her head when she snarls? That is what you need to see if someone does a facial expression too often. When they snarl with their head forward, they are usually angry, as when they pull back it's surprise or very disgusted. If they were to pull their head to the side as they snarl, they may be annoyed, disgusted, or confused.

Alex1986: I have friends that snarl when they are mad, and I know to take a moment before reacting.

Mike1991: That is what my first reaction is when someone shows a snarl. I take two steps back.

John2010: Well, each snarl doesn't mean anger, but yes, take a step back to look at the situation. Don't ask, "What did I do?" Show that you can relate: "I feel that you're upset…" The most likely reply would be, "No, that just didn't feel right…" Or that type of reply. You don't want to promote anger, so if they reply in anger, I'm guessing the best thing to do is to listen.

Tarry1978: Okay, I am seeing that there is more to a look than the look. You need to see how they present the snarl or smile. I have friends that smile too much. I was looking at how she was expressing her smiles, and the smiles did change. I couldn't make a conclusive judgment on it, though.

John2010: Smiles can tell a lot if you know what to look for. I was reading a paper about smiles and it said that if the smile is because of enjoyment, you'll see it in their eyes. This paper talked about the muscles of the eyes and not being able to control them on command. I would suggest paying attention to if the eyes change.

Mike1991: I heard that the truth is in the eyes. I didn't know what that meant, but how would the eyes change?

John2010: That's it. I'm guessing here, but if the eyes don't change, then the smile is a lie. Now, there may be another reason for the eyes not to change. The person may have pinkeye or something wrong that's not as obvious.

Anna1983: When someone blinks too much, that's a dead giveaway.

John2010: What, that they have something in their eye? Rapid eye movement is the giveaway. Blinking is just more noticeable. If someone looks to the side, they may just be thinking.

Tarry1978: Thinking of a lie to say!

John2010: That may be true, but it's the next action that is the tell. If they start using their hands as they talk more, that is a reliable tell. If they start looking around for a thought to drop from thin air, they are lying or looking for a friend to save them.

Alex1986: I've had a lot of experience with posers at the beach and I think I can detect a lie. When they look up too much, it's as if they want to belittle you. They want you to feel as if you are wasting their time pursuing this. Or when they flat-out deny it and act as if it is ridiculous to think they did it they are definitely lying.

John2010: These are things that you find out about particular people, but you shouldn't think everyone that acts like a fibber you once knew is lying. Do you know how to act like you aren't lying?

Mike1991: Look the person in the eye.

Tarry1978: NO, that is when you know something is wrong. There was a girl who was always doing that and I later found out that she was hiding something. I don't know why she couldn't tell us, but she got help. I just wish I knew sooner and could have helped her.

John2010: When I talk to anybody I look them in the eye's or face. It makes them feel that I am interested in what we are talking about. It also makes them feel more secure that I am understanding what they are saying. Keeping your eyes on their face is a good habit to have. Tarry is talking about when someone is staring into your eyes.

Alex1986: Staring into someone's eyes can also show anger, or with a woman, lust. I get that keeping your eyes on the face or looking into the person's eyes is important. At the beach I wear sun glasses a lot, so how else can I help someone feel comfortable around me?

Mike1991: You could talk a lot. I heard that if you carry the conversation, then it will take pressure off them to come up with something to talk about. When I was working with

Nancy on that class project, I talked a lot, because I knew what we were talking about. I can't keep a conversation going when I don't have anything to talk about.

John2010: Okay, the basic idea of communication is to keep the conversation going. The annoying thing is not being able to get a word in edgewise in a group. When you are with an individual or a small subgroup and there is silence and you don't have a common topic to talk about, what should you do? Well, I usually just walk away, but that's not the answer. With a big smile, I say, "Oh, just a few days ago, something ridiculous happed to me…"

Mike1991: What, what happened?

Alex1986: I think we are supposed to fill in the blank.

John2010: Yes, you should be comfortable enough to talk about yourself or a memorable experience you've had, with your friends. I am guessing that you all know when to change the topic of a conversation.

Tarry1978: Yes, change the topic when your friends get bored with it. Jamie gets bored a lot. I think she has adult A.D.D. When I'm talking to her and her eyes start to wonder, I need to get her attention before she fades too much.

Mike1991: Are you sure she's not looking for someone to save her?

Tarry1978: She's not the one who's talking.

John2010: Right, the body language changes and the emotions of the face should be read differently as the interactions proceed. Think of it as offensive or defensive sides of the same field. When you are talking with someone and their eyes aren't on you, that usually means that their mind is wandering. If they've lost interest in what you are talking about, they may be looking for a way to escape.

Tarry1978: I don't want Jamie to want to escape from me.

John2010: I'm sure you don't. If your friends have a common conversation point, then you can use that to gain their attention back. You can also make a short joke or do a play on words on something you are talking about.

Anna1983: I can't do that. My mind doesn't see how to change words or see other meanings of words and make a short joke.

Alex1986: I had a friend who was good at that. He could make jokes out of anything off the top of his head. Of course he had a number of "Your Mother" jokes.

Mike1991: A few of my new friends tell good jokes, but most of them are inappropriate.

John2010: That's why I say keep them short and simple, as in wordplay jokes. Yes, you need to take in account the group you're with before you tell a joke. If your friends are on a team or part of something, you may want to research jokes and witty comments about that.

Tarry1978: Some of the girls I hang out with talk about pop culture, so I should make jokes about people in pop.

Anna1983: They're already made. You just need to find a Web site that specializes in it.

John2010: Yes, do research on-line. A lot of people that you think are just naturals at it have done a lot of research about it.

Mike1991: What's it!

John2010: Enough with the jokes. I got to go. Read you next week.

John logged off, leaving his subjects to their jokes. He rereads tonight's posts and was happy with the response he was getting. John e-mailed all four of the subjects with detailed replies to their weekly posts. He added more information about reading faces and closed with:

I do hope you all are finding these weekly meetings helpful, but you should be doing more on-line research and in-person research on your own.

Family Faces

John took his own advice and went out on Tuesday to observe families in action. He went to the park and saw how different mothers cared for their children. John didn't like what he was seeing, but he guessed that he was cared for in much the same ways.

As John was eating lunch he overheard a couple's conversation and came to the conclusion that they were brother and sister. They were discussing the care of their elderly father. The sister kept implying that the care of her two children was more important than the care of their father. John didn't hear her say so in words, but he read in between the lines or felt that she wanted to put her children first. Her brother caught on, and stormed off saying, "I guess your kids are more important than me too!"

John was thinking about the many encounters he had on Tuesday, but Wednesday night came quickly. He logged on to the blog and posted the information about reading faces from Monday night. John added most of the replies also, because he just hated repeating himself.

John2010: Take your time and read through this information as I read your posts.

John got caught up into the posts and saw the time and rushed to find that Sledge and Rick were chatting about the different faces their wives made.

Rick1982: I've seen Crista smile with me more that she has opened up to me. She smiled before, but she was smiling at me more like that fake smile John told us about.

Sledge1984: Oh yeah, Barb smiles more with her family. I mean, her smiles change more with them. She has that pierced-lips smile, teeth smile, open- mouthed, and giggle, with her family. With me she smiles mostly with a blank stare or like she's not really there. I think that's what John was saying were fake smiles.

Amy1979: Have you noticed a change in how Crista smiles, Rick?

Rick1982: Not really. Crista rarely sows a big smile anymore. She used to smile a lot.

Sledge1984: Well, Barb and I have talked about her family and I hope it was a real laugh after she said that her brother and my sister would make a good couple. I have been trying to read her brother better. These expressions that John told us to look for will help, I hope.

Amy1979: I was thinking of how I smile with Jim and I think I faked it too much.

Sledge1984: Barb doesn't have to fake it with me.

Amy1979: I thought, oh… Well, John says he read a paper that said you can't fake a real smile, but I don't know what he means.

Rick1982: Well, I think it's actually in your eyes. Something like your pupils dilate when it's a real smile. So, I'm guessing if you change your eyes in some way, the smile will look more real, but don't roll your eyes.

Sledge1984: Oh yeah, I hate it when Barb does that. It's like she's belittling me.

Amy1979: I roll my eyes a lot, but I don't mean to belittle Jim.

John2010: Right, it's how you roll your eyes. If you are looking at him and you roll your eyes at him, that is belittling. If you smile, look to the sky, and then to the side as you roll your eyes, you are rolling your eyes at the situation.

Amy1979: Oh, when I read that looking the person in the eye when you talk to them, I thought, *"Yeah, I do that."* Now I see what you were saying, that there is a right way to look at someone, but I don't stare in his eyes.

Sledge1984: Amy, you know how we said you need to be more open with Jim. Well, you need a more open face or a more welcoming look.

John2010: Yes, when you talk with someone, you may need to be thinking of a time when you were happy to gain that expression. If your mind is in a cheerful place and not dreading the conversation, then the encounter will move better. Sledge, do you see yourself treated differently by your brother than your sister? Do they treat each other differently than they treat you? How do you treat each of them, and why? These questions aren't just for Sledge. I want you all to see how you treat each family member and how it differs.

Sledge1984: Well, I treat my brother like a man and… You mean more than that. I'm closer with my sister because we related better throughout our lives and there's the fact that our brother is five years older. Now that we are all adults, I love them the same amount. I still treat him as if he's above me or just further along, and doesn't need me as much. I care for my sister more, I think, because we grew up together.

John2010: Okay, that may have been a bad example. I heard an argument the other day and it sounded as if a sibling was putting care for a brother ahead of another brother. I could see that and imagined how that hurt. You shouldn't make a family member feel less loved, is what I'm getting at. I understand that you may relate with one better than the other, but you should show equal concern.

Amy1979: I see that, but I just see the rest of my family once or twice a year. If I show that I'm overly concerned, then they'll be asking, "What's wrong?"

Rick1982: Well, I have felt detached from my brother and we never related very well. I have tried to connect with Joe over the years. I should try that emotional communication with him.

Sledge1984: Showing concern is important. Barb's father does that good. I think that is why he is so good at getting what he wants from anyone. All he does is show interest or concern in what the other person is doing.

John2010: Amy, you should e-mail a family member and tell them something that has happened in your recent life and ask what they're up to. Just showing interest can broaden your connection with your family. I know they have their lives, but let them know you're concerned.

Rick1982: I've been thinking about my brother recently, but it feels like Joe pushes me away. I don't know, maybe it's me. Our conversations are just too blunt and to the point. Maybe I should try that emotional communication and show concern, because we are not kids anymore.

Sledge1984: That's what I thought, but Barb's brother still acts like a kid. I tried emotional communication with him and he told Barb that I was coming on to him.

Amy1979: Well, some guys think that girls are the only ones that can be emotional. I thought you were thinking he was gay.

Sledge1984: I just thought Andy was getting too close at times. I guess I just don't like to be touched that much.

Rick1982: I never had that problem with my brother. He is just two years older, which, yes, through the teen years you have to expect us to be in separate places. We just never connected, even after Joe graduated from college. I really thought he would help me, but anyway, after college I tried to bond with him. Joe just belittled me like John said with his eyes.

John2010: You need to find something in common or find anything he likes and use it to connect with him.

Sledge1984: Yes, like Barb's father, show concern and use it to open him up to you. Call his wife and find out what's happening in his life.

Rick1982: She will tell him I called and that will put him on guard. Joe is a bit controlling of his wife and she can't keep anything from him. At the last family gathering, she actually started to cry when he was just asking her why she hid something. It was a surprise for Joe, but if she is that on edge, then I can't expect her to keep anything from him.

Amy1979: Why is she so scared of him?

Rick1982: Oh, she's not. It's just that she can be too dramatic.

John2010: Rick, you have taken apart his childhood. You should look at his adulthood to see how his childhood affected his life. You all can find how to affect your siblings' lives now by looking at their childhoods.

Amy1979: I have looked at my childhood and saw how I was affected by my two brothers, but I don't really care how they were affected.

John2010: Amy, I'm sure that how you affected their lives affected how you were affected by them. If you don't really care, "your words," how things affect you...

Sledge1984: I think Amy is just worried about controlling Jim.

Amy1979: I just don't see how it matters.

John2010: It's all connected. I really wanted to point out that it matters how you treat people. In particular your family. Because they are family, you don't love one more than the other. You can get along better with one, but you should show equal concern. Amy, if you don't even e-mail each other, then they don't see that you care. I understand if you aren't a part of their lives, but it is important that they know you're thinking of them.

Rick1982: I have been thinking of my brother a lot since I've taken apart his life in those jars of life. I'm starting to miss him.

Amy1979: Well, from what I get from your weekly posts he is too controlling, Rick, and I don't mean like me. I'm worried and just like to know what's going on in Jim's life. I'm getting that I can't be involved with every part of it. We are talking more now that I'm listening more, and that really makes a difference.

Sledge1984: Yes, I have listened to my sister more and I think she's lonely. I think that is why she has been spending time with Barb and her family. I hate to think that she wanted to spend time with me and I wasn't there. I'm using emotional communication with her and we are talking more.

Amy1979: Sledge, that's bad, to feel you weren't there for someone. How can I tell when someone feels lonely?

John2010: If the way they carry themselves changes. You should carry your shoulders high to show confidence. A depressed person will be slouching. Now these changes you should be able to notice, but you need to know how this person carry's themselves.

Sledge1984: I guess I should have seen my sisters depression, but I don't see her every day and I didn't know to see how she was carrying herself.

Rick1982: Right, you shouldn't think everyone who doesn't carry their shoulders high is depressed. Just don't think they're confident. Crista rarely shows confidence, but she isn't depressed, I don't think.

John2010: That's right, Rick you need to see Crista for who she is. You three have been doing great at getting to know your family better. I am glad that you are making headway, but I think you should look deeper to see how you have affected your family. You can use what you learn in how to affect your family now. Your friends and coworkers are your extended family, so you may want to look deeper in these relationships also.

John left the blog with his subjects chatting about which friends or coworkers were most like their family members. He reviewed their weekly posts and thought of how he should help them next week. John thought he should add something about good posture in this email.

People that have an upright posture have more confidence in their own thoughts. However, people who assumed a slumped over with a less confident posture, don't have much confidence in their selves.

For more information about confident posture please search for research on the World Wide Web.

Faces at Work

John was thinking of how to read faces at work, so he read about encounters at work. John found a story that he thought was relevant to finding out how some one feels. This fictional story was about odd faces and how hard it is not to judge these people. These faces were so distorted that they always looked happy, sad, cross-eyed, in pain, or surprised.

After John finished this story, he was laughing, but could see the lessons in it. John thought of how to incorporate these lessons in the meeting. He considered telling them the story, but he thought, *They would just laugh.*

Friday night came quickly, but John thought he was ready and logged on early, or so he thought.

John2010: I see you three got here early too. I haven't read your weekly posts yet, but I see what you are discussing. I wanted to talk about faces and how to read them tonight, but I think first I'd like to let you all know how reinforcing writing can be. I see that you are complaining about people at work. Well, trust me, the more complaining, the worse you'll feel.

John2010: I'm sure you may feel relieved to find people that are in the same situation you are. In the long run, it is best to do something about these people. I've mentioned subtle ways of going about it, and I may touch on this again next week. It is important to read these people's faces before approaching them at work.

Jill1959: I think I can tell when not to approach this girl, because she is about to have one of her fits.

John2010: Why is she having a fit? What kind of fit is it or will it be? Does she cry? Does she hold all her tears in until she gets home? All I'm saying is that you need to see more in her than the fit.

Jill1959: Now I feel bad!

Sally1974: Oh, that's okay, but if one of your friends has a fit, then you may want to look into it.

Bill4267: Well, people like this are annoying, so if you could use emotional communication to get it through to her that it's not okay, you should.

John2010: That's right, but you may want to take notice of her facial expression before and after each fit. The fit is to hide feelings more than anything else.

Timmy1982: That girl sounds like a real cow, but I was reading your post, and Jill, it sounds like you are making good friends at work. I have made some new friends, but I don't know how good they are. Sometimes they can be more draining than those two guys that I need to get to work together. I have changed how I'm working with them.

John2010: That's good. Why don't you four share how you've all changed how you treat people at work, while I read through your weekly posts?

Bill4267: Okay, I guess I've been talking with more people at work. In the past I've kept to myself mostly. Most of all, I see how much effort it takes, which is why I haven't bothered. I noticed that two of my bosses were looking me over the other day after I was using emotional communication with a girl at work. You can read about it in my post, but at the end of the day one of these men talked to me. I don't talk to this boss, I talk to the head of my group and he talks to this boss.

Jill1959: I skimmed the post when I saw you showed up here, but I never thought you to be shy. I jumped to the conclusion, you wouldn't do anything like that. I can see why that boss would want to talk to you.

Timmy1982: I would have just backed away, but that was good how you related to her situation.

Bill4267: I couldn't relate, but I have had situations that upset me, because I was confused.

Jill1959: Bill, don't just think she is confused. I like that you got her to open up.

Bill4267: I didn't mean to. The boss that talked to me later settled my mind. He told me she got the help she needed. I tried to tell him that I was just practicing on her, but he didn't get that. He told me to come to this weekend's meeting.

Timmy1982: I wouldn't be caught dead at a group counseling like that. With my coworkers all there.

Sally1974: I just finished reading that and I think it's cool how the president of your company is getting into the New Age treatments.

Timmy1982: I'm not into those New Age things.

Sally1974: What do you think this is? Anyway, how is your team working out?

Timmy1982: I think one of those guys is on to me. He gave me a look three times like he could see under the curtain. I used emotional communication or emotional manipulation and he didn't like it.

Bill4267: Just ignore those thoughts. If he has a problem he'll let you know.

John2010: That's right, but now I would like to start talking about reading faces. I fond a list of things to look for when people are beginning to lie that I found.

Here's the top eight list of suspicious behaviors:

- A change in the voice's pitch.
- A change in the rate of speech.
- A sudden increase in the number of "ums" and "ahs."
- A change in eye contact. Normally, one makes eye contact one-quarter to one-half of the time. If suddenly, at the convenient moment to lie, he's staring at you or looking away, beware.
- Turning his body away from you, even if just slightly.
- Suddenly being able to see the white on the top and bottom of a person's eyes, not just the sides.
- A hand reaching, even if momentarily, to cover part of the face, especially the mouth.
- Nervous movement of feet or legs.

John also posted the information and the replies from the other two nights that he thought were relevant. Then John thought how he was to introduce how to read a fixed face, as in when someone always wears a smile or a kind of snarl.

Timmy1982: I'm glad you cut all of those expressions down to four. You say that any one expression may mean something different for another person. How do you know?

John2010: Well, how long have you worked with these coworkers? Wait, that question was for everyone. Now, you can categorize people by how they dress, and you can use those categories to get a general feel for how someone will express themself. There are people that always, or at least around you, wear a snarl of some kind.

John2010: If you know anybody like this, you shouldn't read it as how they feel. You need to look for those small changes in how they express themselves.

Jill1959: How will we know if we should find out why they are snarling, like Tarry wishes she did?

Sally1974: Yeah, but I'm guessing Tarry's friend changed from looking a different way, and that's what you need to look for. Like that joke, if you keep making that face, it may just stick. If somebody is snarling a lot, then you may want to use a short comment to see her reaction. Then use emotional communication to find what's going on.

Bill4267: That's what happened. That girl that usually is smiling, I saw she wasn't, so I thought I could practice emotional communication on her. Really it was because I thought she noticed me looking at her too much.

John2010: A good way to approach anyone is by showing concern. That was good how you showed the concern with this girl that you haven't talked to before. You pointed out how she grew a smile as you said hi to her, but how did she change throughout the exchange? In your post you pointed out the drastic changes, but you should write about the minor changes also.

Bill4267: There were a lot of changes in her that hour.

Jill1959: I'm sure, but I think John wants you to see the changes in her expressions that led up to those drastic changes.

Timmy1982: I have noticed that it doesn't take much to see that someone has changed during the exchanges I've had recently. It's just hard to see what these changes mean.

Sally1974: I know what you mean, but the men at work are easy to read unless something's wrong. They try to hide it. This week one guy was showing distress, so I went up to him and started to use emotional communication. When I hit it he started to talk, but then I think he thought he was being too girly and just straightened up. He told me not to worry my pretty head about it and to concentrate on my work.

John2010: That sounds like a good encounter to write about, not for us but for you. When you write about encounters with coworkers, it will help you. If you write every facial and body movement down, you will know what to look for next time. Bill and everyone else should write down emotional encounters with strangers also. When you see these expressions in anybody else, you will know what your next move should be.

Bill4267: I've tried to remember how I have reacted with my wives, but it's always different, how I remember each encounter.

John2010: Yes, there are differences in the implication of every encounter. Use emotional communication in the encounter to find how to react, but the common reaction is usually the right one. With friends or someone you are manipulating, you may want to learn more before you react.

Jill1959: I don't want to manipulate anyone.

Timmy1982: Well, then how are you going to get ahead at work?

Jill1959: I just don't like feeling like I was being devious towards anyone.

John2010: Good point, but Timmy has a good point also. Use emotional communication to get closer with someone at work to gain a new outlook and get ahead. You are using these people as they are using you, to gain something.

Jill1959: Okay, I have gained. I think people are looking at me differently at work. I think it's because I use the emotional communication and I think of how I want to be treated.

Sally1974: That's right, you should treat everybody as you wish to be treated. When I think I see someone has changed, I try to see why and start staring at them too much. I think those notes on reading our coworkers' faces will help me a lot.

Bill4267: People have started to interact with me more. Not just because of that girl, but before that I had noticed it. I think that gave me more confidence and I started to talk more. I mean, a month ago I would have just sat and wondered about that girl.

Timmy1982: It usually takes a while for me to talk with new people. With emotional communication I open up more with people and I think they are being more open with me. That new team I'm working with has been moving along easier as I use the emotional communication to try and relate.

John2010: That is great to hear. Tonight let's leave it at that and I will attach that story I found about faces to the e-mail. I'll give you a link to an on-line encyclopedia that has real faces and what they mean.

John logged off with a smile, thinking, *It sounds like I'm really helping these people.*

On Saturday, John was feeling good and thought that he should go out and do some real-world research. He went to a nearby mall to find people to socialize with. When John got to the mall, he looked around and saw couples and small groups together. *I guess most people come to the mall with friends. I sure feel lonely.*

John was thinking, *Should I just find a seat or find a group to join before lunch?*

He guessed that the best way to meet a group that he might like would be at a music store. A person's choice of music says a lot about their character, so John headed for the nearby CD shop.

John saw a group of three, two girls and a man, who looked to be in their mid-twenties. They were talking about music that John knew a bit about, so he said hi.

"I heard that the lead singer of that band is having some girl trouble."

"I don't know how. He looks like he has plenty of choices."

With a twisted smile from who John assumed was his girlfriend, the man got a shot in the arm. They all laughed and talked about bands as John made it a point to flirt with the other girl. John had someone to eat lunch with, and not long after they finished they parted ways.

Emotional Friends

John had found some more information that he had already shared at each meeting. He felt that he should make a point of the different types of people that they might find. On Monday morning he was reviewing his notes of the day before. On Sunday John went to an exhibit that had all kinds of characters.

At this exhibit, there were loud people, quiet people, and enablers. John wrote notes about these people and took account of the events. The events that he was looking at started to be the overdramatic people. He found that the quiet people were being dramatic in their own way. When the quiet people would speak up, their friends would listen better to them. The friends listened to the people that were always loud with less interest. The overdramatic people would get ignored more than listened to at times.

John did notice that there were more enablers than anything else. The enablers were the people that engaged with the dramatic people just for the show. John liked to think that most of them meant well. He saw that most people just wanted to be heard, but John just rolled his eyes. Of course these enablers didn't realize these people were looking for help.

Monday night came quickly and John logged on to find the four subjects of the friends group reading each other's posts.

John2010: I found a story that I thought pointed out how the little things in people's lives can affect them. Now, these little things are things that you personally may not see as life changing. After you have all finished reading each other's posts, please read this story:

There was a lounge room in an office building that had two sets of coffee mugs to choose from. One of these sets was 12 oz. white mugs. The other set had five pairs of 10 oz. mugs of different colors. A woman that worked in an office in this office building by this lounge would open the white cabinet to see a rainbow of colors to choose from. This woman would always choose a blue coffee mug that reminded her of the sky outside.

One day this woman came into work, went to the white lounge, and opened the white cabinet door to find a new set of white 12 oz. coffee mugs. She looked around the cabinet, stood on her tiptoes, but couldn't find the rainbow. She chose a white 12 oz. mug, added coffee, took it to her office, put it on her white coffee mug heater, and sat down. With a feeling of disappointment she started her day, and throughout her day she felt that something was missing.

At the end of the day she looked at the empty white coffee mug that sat on her white coffee mug heater that had been off since two. She took this empty white coffee mug to the white sink in the white lounge and took a breath. As she pulled her car out of the underground garage, she looked in between two buildings and up. She took a pause as she looked at the sky and felt a smile growing. She thought to herself, "I miss you, sky." She took a breath. That's what was wrong today.

This woman stopped at the dollar parlor on her way home and found a shelf full of different-colored coffee mugs. She bought four blue 10 oz. coffee mugs and the next day she took them to her office with her. She put three blue 10 oz. coffee mugs into a drawer in her desk in her office. She took one blue 10 oz. coffee mug to the white lounge and poured herself a cup of coffee.

This woman took her blue 10 oz. coffee mug back to her office, to her desk, and set it on her white coffee mug heater. As she took a seat, she looked around her office with her eyes being drawn to her blue coffee mug, and smiled.

John2010: I hope you liked this story. It shows how one little thing can change the entire day of the person you are trying to affect. Now, I hope I've emphasized the need to read people's day-by-day actions. We've talked about emotional intelligence and how to use it, but with overemotional people you need to be careful. We should talk about your role in these situations and not being an enabler.

Anna1983: I found that I am an enabler with Patty, but I have tried to be more emotionally aware of her and Scott. Scott started to tease me when I started showing more interest in him, but I got mad. I don't like it when people point out my emotions, and he was wrong. We were alone at this time, so I let him have it and it came out wrong. Not too wrong, but he threw it back at me with a comment like, Oh, so you have a crush on Patty now.

Mike1991: One of my new friends is always doing that, but as a joke. When somebody fumbles their words, he picks it up and makes a joke. People have just rolled their eyes at him most of the time, but I have watched him to see what he sees. John did tell us to look for people that are more aware.

John2010: Yes, that's good, watch him and learn what he is watching for. Mike, I have to warn you not to use humor to gain friends. Yes, funny people tend to have a lot of friends, but most people really don't get the joke. From what I've read in your post, it sounds like you are trying to join two different groups. It looks good how you stood up for Nancy against Jay and you gained respect.

Mike1991: I don't know about respect, but some people are looking at me differently.

Tarry1978: Yeah, you're not a pushover anymore! I'm not saying you were, but now more people know it. I think some of Jamie's new friends think of me as just being a tagalong that they can walk all over.

Alex1986: Tarry, I've had that problem a number of times. When you join a new group, it takes time to prove yourself. When you have a friend in this group, then everybody thinks of you as your friends friend. They look to your friend to see how to treat you, but when she is too engaged with these other friends you need to represent yourself. Don't start by telling off the leader of the pack, like Mike did.

Mike1991: What I… Well, I didn't tell him off. I just told him to stop it. In an abrupt manner.

Anna1983: Oh, I hate it when Patty takes what I did and overdramatizes it.

John2010: Well, let's be friendly. I wanted to show you how not to be an enabler for these emotional people. What Mike did was good to show them that he didn't like being treated that way. I would suggest going about it by starting with a question. As in Anna's situation with Scot, in like situations you shouldn't straight-out deny it. You could ask why they would think something so absurd. When you deny something so abruptly, the person who you are denying could ask himself why so defensive?

Tarry1978: Now, John, that story about the blue mug. I have found some little meaningless things about Jamie in the collage I made, but I don't want to hurt her.

John2010: Tarry, you could take one of these things away and replace it with you somehow. Now, you don't want Jamie to know that she lost this thing because of you. I've told you to get to know the people around the person you are trying to change and use them to affect this person.

Mike1991: I have done that with Nancy's friends, but I just used them to work together. I used that emotional communication with one guy and he got the other guys to back off.

Alex1986: Right, I read that in your post. I just hope you didn't do it as obviously as you made it sound. I have some friends from school and I used one guy much like you did. Well, he was talking with his girlfriend about it and she made a statement that clued him in on my scheme. He got hurt. I tried to tell him not to listen to her, but he wouldn't speak with me for months.

Anna1983: I wouldn't like anyone to use my emotions to take advantage of me.

Alex1986: The thing is that I wasn't taking advantage of him. I just used him to take advantage of another guy.

John2010: That is why you need to take consideration of all the outcomes. When you use emotional communication, you need to take in account how it would make you feel. Of course, no one likes to be used, so as Alex said, don't be too obvious.

Tarry1978: Jamie's new friends are all overemotional, but I think I kind of connected with one. She speaks her mind much as I do, just louder. I think I can just mention to her about the annoying things about her other friends and she'll say something.

Anna1983: That's good, just let them know. Oh, and you aren't really friends with this girl, so you don't care about hurting her feelings. You should, because what if Jamie likes her?

Tarry1978: Oh, right, thanks. Jamie wouldn't like seeing her hurt. I don't like her for a different reason, so I can point out things to her about these other girls and she'll say something. Jamie may hear her and listen to her better than she has been listening to me. I just hope she says the right things.

John2010: That's right, you never know exactly how people will respond. When people get overemotional, I have found it may be best to respond with a question. An emotional person can take any comment as an attack, so I think it's best to make them think. You can ask them about the problem that they are having and that may get them to think that it's not such a problem.

Alex1986: I have made a list about my girlfriend and her two best friends. I have found how they act just before they explode. Well, Jessie is the one who explodes. The other two are just enablers. When I see them starting to get that look,

I just take cover and get a defensive posture. You are saying that I should ask Jessie about what's wrong, so she doesn't get the chance to go off.

John2010: It's how you go about it. I know that when you see that she is getting upset, you just want to roll your eyes and say, "…" You want to use the emotional communication to make her think you understand and ask why. You may want to start, "I'm sorry this is upsetting, but why… ?" Stating that you know her feelings can be a good opening, but be careful you don't act like you know more than her.

Tarry1978: Oh, I hate that, when one of Jamie's new friends does that. She acts like she knows what's going on in your mind, and she really doesn't have a clue. It's not just me; she does this with everyone and it's annoying just to watch.

Mike1991: But you do watch. I was thinking about being an enabler, and just watching, having a reaction is a way that you are an enabler. We all do it!

John2010: Mirroring their actions is a good way to react with no real reaction. If this person is acting stupidly or inappropriately, seeing you act the same way can defuse the situation.

Tarry1978: Oh yeah, that was so funny when I was out with Jamie and her new friends. One of them did something that was upsettingly stupid. Another friend there started doing the same thing, and instead of being upset we all started laughing.

Alex1986: When I read about that I couldn't stop laughing. I remembered how I had a friend one summer that would do that, but I remember him as being mean about it.

Anna1983: Right. Well, I don't want to be looked at as being mean…

John2010: Yes, humor can be taken as being mean, so with new friends you may want to make an effort not to be funny. Use the emotional communication, and when you find anyone is showing you that they are upset, show that you understand where they are coming from.

John ended the night with that and hoped that these subjects understood how not to be an enabler of bad habits. He read the posts about his subjects' week again and found that Alex was making lists about his family also. Alex was finding ways to work out some problems that he had been having with his sister. In the e-mail that John sent Alex, he asked him to join the family group on Wednesday.

As John was reading Mike's post, he saw how Mike was using his new friends to affect each other. John didn't feel that Mike was aware of what he was bringing to these two groups. He started to write the e-mail to Mike with directions of how to make it work, but he stopped himself. John just wrote how he saw the situation was turning out.

Anna's post was telling John that she was scared to take advantage of her friends. John tried to reassure her that using emotional communication would show her friends that she cared more and didn't just want to use them.

John felt that Tarry was looking for a way to become more of a part of Jamie's life. He saw that Tarry was doing a good job with the collages, and taking apart her new friends' lives to find where to strike. John was feeling proud of his new friends. Then he remembered that they were just strangers that he was using as subject-matter for his new book.

Engaging the Family

On Tuesday morning John thought about last night's meeting with the friends group. He hoped that he emphasized the point of not being too overwhelmed by emotional friends. John had had experiences much like Alex's where a friend came to the conclusion that he was just being used, because of overthinking the situation. An old girlfriend of John's got him to stop showing his arrogance as much. That was what got John to research emotional communications.

John was thinking of how hard it was not to feel above his sister and had learned not to state his thoughts around her. Before breakfast Tuesday morning, John searched online for information about family engagements. Most of the information that he found was about dysfunctional families, but John did find some useful examples. He thought of going out to watch families and how they interacted. John thought it might be a bit disturbing seeing a single man watching you and your children, so he stayed in.

By Wednesday evening, John thought he was ready for the meeting with the family group. He did hope that Alex would join them tonight, because John found that some of Alex's insights were helpful. After John logged in, he found Amy and Sledge chatting while Rick was reading the posts.

Amy1979: After reading how Sledge has been interacting with his wife's family, I think I see how easy it can be if we just change our approach.

Sledge1984: Right, I have been more forward with my wife's father and now it doesn't seem that he or I need to make such an effort. We are laughing more, and even spending time with Andy isn't as draining.

John2010: I was just reading how humor can diffuse a dysfunctional family. I just told the friend groups not to use humor to attract friends, because there will be more people that don' t get it than that do. With your family, humor is good, because you usually know what makes your family laugh.

Rick1982: Sledge found how to control Andy with humor, but he can't keep using the same joke.

Amy1979: Right, and that joke can be belittling.

John2010: Most jokes are, but I'm glad you mentioned that, because this new knowledge about people can make you arrogant. Let's talk more about using emotional communication and how to use it. I see that Sledge has used it to be more involved with his step family, but it can backfire.

Rick1982: Sledge, if Andy finds out how you bent that one girl's view of him, he won't trust you.

Amy1979: Oh, I hoped that was a lie.

Sledge1984: What, I told her how he treats all women.

John2010: Sledge, I don't think you've seen how he treats all women, but let's not linger. I invited Alex again to share some views on how to use the little things, and I like his views on relationships.

Sledge1984: Humor is a great way to be included if you have the right audience. I didn't think what I was saying was really all that funny, but Jeff had a kick.

Amy1979: I try to be funny with my husband, but I actually feel like I have to dumb down or he doesn't get it. He likes sit-com humor, but sit-coms don't have much of a story to them.

Sledge1984: That's what makes them so fun to watch. You don't need to put much thought into it.

Rick1982: I don't need to put much thought into making fun of my wife, but that isn't productive. I have realized that when I listen more I feel like rolling my eyes at her a lot, but I don't. Now that I am paying attention to how I speak to her, I think I used to look down on her and her opinions.

Amy1979: Oh, that's bad. I wasn't looking down on Jim, but I think I was taking him for granted and not seeing how he has changed. We are talking more and I see him making an effort to talk with me. I have found a hobby to do, so I'm not looking over him as much. I'm keeping myself busy.

John2010: Yes, seriously, that is good that you all have seen that if you change a little, it has a big effect on the person you are trying to change. Now that you are finding out the things that make these people who they are, you can see the little things in their lives that will change them. You may want to change them in a different way now that is better.

Alex1986: I have just finished reading this week's posts and, Sledge, I'd just like to point out one thing. You are spending more time with your wife's family. What does your wife really think about that?

Sledge1984: She seems happy about it. She has said that her father is rubbing off on me.

Alex1986: Is that a good thing? Is the time she's spending with her mother and sister good? Do you want them to rub off on her? In last week's post you were complaining about them…

Rick1982: Alex is right, I'm lucky that my wife's family lives over a hundred miles away. Oh, and she can't stand them either.

Alex1986: I used to have a girlfriend that was hanging out at my house when I was away with the guys, and she started to change. I have two younger sisters that started to rub off on her, and before the end of the summer it was like I was dating all three of them.

Sledge1984: I don't want to date Barb's sister, or her mom for that matter.

Amy1979: Right, I didn't want to be married to a drunk, so I didn't like that Jim was going to the bars every night after work. He has been coming home more after work. I think it's because I started that hobby and I'm not right there to question him.

John2010: That's good, Amy, but is that all you wanted to change about Jim?

Amy1979: No!

Alex1986: Amy, you may want to think about how you are changing your husband, because if you change him too much he won't be the same person. One summer my friend made me feel betrayed, because of how he was trying to change me. He was collaborating with a longtime girlfriend of mine and they were sharing information. Now, this girl knew things about me that I wouldn't share with my best friend. All I'm saying is to use what you know wisely, and don't use the most private things.

Rick1982: I was listening to my wife's chattering and I brought up a private matter that I wanted to talk with her about, but she thought it had to do with what she was saying. She gave me a strange look that put me in defense mode right away. I drew back and after she said, "What?" I realized it and just started, "No, no, no." It took almost five minutes, but she did end up laughing at the situation.

Amy1979: Alex, that girl doesn't sound like a good friend.

Alex1986: She is my neighbor at the beach and we've been on and off for years. I have since forgiven her.

John2010: Yes, that is good. With these skills you may run across some information that could hurt you or hurt the ones you love, so you need to use emotional communication and take things in stride. I don't think I need to repeat that you shouldn't use private personal things to change the ones you love.

Sledge1984: I am close with my sister and I use those things against her all the time.

Amy1979: And you wonder why she hasn't been sharing as much with you.

Sledge1984: I just think her new friends don't like me. We laughed last week when we talked about them.

Alex1986: Yeah, I was thinking about that. Why do you care about her new friends so much?

Sledge1984: Like my brother-in-law, the two guys are flirting too much.

Amy1979: Aren't they that girl Rebecca's boyfriends?

Sledge1984: That is what I'm worried about, my sister getting caught in a quadrangle. And then, how safe is the sex with someone who you know isn't just with you?

Amy1979: When your sister told you that they thought you were a prude, did you tell her why you thought they thought that?. I can see that they are swingers and you aren't that type, so did you tell her that you are concerned?

Sledge1984: Almost, but she rolled her eyes and started to turn away. I thought I might be pushing her away.

John2010: I didn't want to bring this up, but let's talk about defensive communication. It may help with emotional communication that you can't relate to. Now, Sledge, in your post you wrote that Rebecca was using verbal abuse against you and it made you feel bad. There are some good tactics as in quick comebacks or mocking them that may help you feel better. I suggest using those tactics quickly after they attack you, but don't become the attacker.

Rick1982: Defensive communication for me is just saying I'm sorry and trying to get my wife to understand that I didn't mean what she thought.

Amy1979: Yeah, that takes five minutes.

Alex1986: Just don't show that you're getting defensive. Rick, it may have been easier to show humor than sorrow.

John2010: That's right, there are many ways to hide defensiveness. The best way is with a smile. When people use verbal abuse and you don't have a witty comeback, you can look confused and say, "I thought that was the way you liked it…" You can shape that sentence as you wish, but the pause of confusion is important. It gives you time to think of what to say, and the people around you gain interest in your confusion.

Amy1979: Okay, I have a friend at work who is made fun of, behind her back mostly. I don't like it, so I should speak up. I shouldn't attack them; I should turn their joke around on them.

Alex1986: What about that blue coffee mug story? I have looked closer at my friends and enemies and I have found mugs for most of them. I can see how to disorient these people and then come in to comfort them enough, so I'm on their good side.

John almost forgot about the story. He posted it with the best responses that the friends group had. Alex explained how to make it look as if someone else did the dirty work. Then to be there when this person needed you.

Amy thought of a way to use this by just making Jim believe he was missing something that made Alex warn her yet again. Sledge was finding ways to communicate with his sister and avoid the abuse from her friends. This meeting ran long, but John stayed with them to make sure they remembered to smile to put people at ease.

Enabling at Work

John did some research about habits and how they affect coworkers before he logged on to the blog. John found all of the subjects were busy reading each other's posts, so he took a glance through the posts.

John found that Timmy was using the emotional communication well with his new team of workers. Bill was interacting with different people at work and learning to be more social. John thought about what Bill was looking to get out of these meetings and he glanced again at Bill's post.

John2010: I see that you are all making good progress at work, but, Bill, have you changed the views of the men in your office? I see that you're connecting with other people in the building, but are you working on how you can use them?

Bill4267: I just finished reading Timmy's post, and he's getting himself into trouble. I have been making my lists better and learning things about my coworkers. I found out my head manager interacts with one of the men I've been talking with him at the bar on the other side of town. I hope he gives me a good assessment if he mentions me to him.

John2010: Give this man a reason to speak highly of you. If your boss or manager hears good things about you from anyone outside of your office, group, or team, he may gain a better view of you, but he may not if the review is of something you do with your boss or team.

Sally1974: Right, I get it. You want to show your heads a different side of you. You need to act a certain way on the job, but if you can show them that there is more to you, they can have a more rounded view of you.

Timmy1982: That's what those annoying outings are for. I guess it is good for your boss to see that you are more than what you are in the office.

Jill1959: Right, I've heard some of the girls I have been going out with talking around the office about me, and I've seen coworkers look at me differently. Just this week a girl that I've seen around, but was kind of avoiding me, came right up to me to ask for help on her PC. I remember when I had no idea how to use a PC. What I was doing was trying to make this girl comfortable as I was explaining how to use the program. I think being more social with the other girls has helped my confidence, and now I'm sharing more.

Sally1974: In your post you said that one of the girls told this woman about a brief conversation you had with her about that program. That tells us that any good communication with a coworker or an extension of that from work can help change how you are looked upon at work.

Bill4267: John, I've been spending time with my coworkers at lunch trying to learn more about them, but most of what they talk about is sports and complaints. I've added these things to my notes, but all I get out of that are the bad things in their lives.

John2010: That's good, you can bond over those things. You should look for the few good things also to use to make change. I have a story that I shared with the other groups about how a little thing as small as a different-colored mug can affect someone.

John told the story and gave them the feedback he got from the other groups. They looked closer at their situations and Timmy needed help.

Timmy1982: Now my team must think I'm a dork. I told you what happened in my post. I thought it was going well, but I didn't see that these two men work better together and I pulled them apart.

Sally1974: I thought what you did was good. How you put your foot down and gained respect.

Bill4267: I think Timmy sees how he didn't need that right now, and he could have kept the team together.

Sally1974: They are. It's just those two boys who aren't working as closely.

John2010: I think that's the team Bill's talking about. I don't want to tell you, Timmy, how to do your business, but I see you getting two separate campaigns again.

Timmy1982: I did and I had to merge them myself. The head didn't seem too impressed. I have another week to get it all done, but I'm going to have to get these guys working together.

Jill1959: Have you spoken with that girl who has worked with them before?

Timmy1982: Not today, but I think she was trying to let me know these two usually work better together. Yeah, she said that exact thing, but at the time I just rolled my eyes at her. On Monday when we meet I'm going to have a talk with those two.

Bill4267: Be careful, no one likes to be singled out. I would never blame myself, but since you are the head of this team, I think a way to go about this is to straight-out say, "It's my fault."

Sally1974: I just looked at Timmy's post, and after making the effort of gaining their respect I don't know that blaming himself is the best way of going about this. I would take these two separately and tell them that how they acted last week won't be tolerated.

John2010: Well, what Sally is saying will not stop them from thinking you're a dork, but that is a way. I just think they'll think you're a hard-ass instead. Maybe you want that, but the friendly leader gets more feedback from his team. Blaming yourself can get you a lot of respect.

Jill1959: It takes a strong man to say that he's wrong.

Timmy1982: I can do that...

Sally1974: You weren't wrong to want this team to listen to you.

John2010: Sally is right: you didn't do anything wrong. You just didn't get the outcome you wanted. You can take the team and say, "This isn't working. We need to get organized and we all need to work together." Then the team will look at each other and I would be surprised if one of them doesn't make a suggestion. If one of these two men says, "I can't work with him," you will have to put your foot down before he walks out. Then you need to unite them. Give them each a compliment on how their work has been great, then get them to see how it wouldn't have been great if they weren't working together.

Timmy1982: I don't like being the man, but I do see how Sally's advice would be good if I was the controlling type. I like it when I feel that I can add to the team without being shut down by the boss. In this case I'm playing that role, so I can see how I should make the team feel welcome. Last week, I hope, I showed these guys that I will put them in their place when I feel I need to.

Bill4267: I can see that in a team dynamic, John's way would be best. I haven't had many jobs that worked in teams, so I think that's why I may think that Sally's idea is good. If I have subordinates that I need to work together like Timmy may have, then I would have to make a plan to keep the control of the subordinates.

Jill1959: Good point. I have had a job where my boss had so much trouble keeping his thoughts straight, he started keeping a notebook. If I had the responsibility of keeping a team organized, I would have a notebook of how they act and how they respond and the group dynamic that I'm trying to have.

Timmy1982: I have the lists of who these people are in folders designated by groups. I can start notes of each group and my plans for them. Yeah, that would be good for all of us to do, to keep notes of how we want to change each group.

John2010: Yes, good, all of you… You can have notes about what you want to change in each group. You can look at the lists about each person's life and see what little things you can change to get closer to what you want.

Jill1959: I have gained the respect from most of my coworkers. I think they see me as less of a burden and more of a team player that they can benefit from knowing. I don't know if I said that right.

Sally1974: I get it, I have made some progress with that, but some men still see me as a ditsy girl. That guy that I finely went out for a drink with says that some people he works with see that I've changed.

Timmy1982: That's right, you said you may be promoted.

Sally1974: I think he was kidding. He said it wasn't a date but he was flirting with me all evening.

Jill1959: Were you okay with that? I see some guys flirting a lot because that's just who they are. It doesn't mean a thing, but even if it's not at work you should tell him how it makes you feel.

Timmy1982: If a guy flirted too much with me I just wouldn't go out with him after work anymore.

Bill4267: Anybody likes to be flirted with. Jill is right, because it can get inappropriate fast with some guys. I'm guessing that he just had coffee, which is good because it's less likely that he'll get carried away.

Sally1974: I did start dreaming about getting that promotion, but an image came to me of him laughing and saying, "I can't believe that ditsy girl thought I was serious." It would be nice if I could, so do you think I should write a note to myself to try to get promoted?

Timmy1982: You should always work with that expectation. You can find the thing that you need to change to get that promotion, and find the little things to change what will get you closer to that promotion.

John2010: It looks like it's going well for all of you… I just wanted to make sure I pointed out that the habits that people have is something to look for and add to the lists. Watch out for your habits, because they may be holding you back. Sally, the reason that people think you are ditzy may be the habits that you have developed. Habits are learned and they happen to make you comfortable. They give you something to do besides worrying, most of the time. I was promoting that you find a hobby to connect with coworkers outside of work. Hobbies can replace bad habits also. Now, what are bad habits?

Sally1974: Aren't they all?

John2010: Well, they all can be taken advantage of by someone else who knows of your habits. All habits are good when you start them, or you wouldn't start them. Habits make you comfortable, and when you rely on them they can become costly. Now, to change the opinion that someone has of you, you may just need to stop or change some of your habits. For next week try to make a list of your habits and grade them by pointing out the ones you can do without. Remember, habits are things you're good at. New habits are good if you choose them.

After that posting, John let the subjects chat about their habits and how to change them as he rereads tonight's posts. He wrote a general e-mail stating that their progress looked good and thanking them for their input. John thought he should include in to nights email how important affirmation is.

John was more specific with his comments about their specific posts, and he gave more details on what to do. He had to remember to acknowledge that these were just suggestions of a way to do it with each comment. John had learned that people don't like to be told what to do or that how they are doing things is wrong. He also didn't want to be blamed if his suggestions didn't work.

John was remembering how he used to be orderly with how he communicated. That did make him look like he was confident and knew what he was doing, but John also remembered specific times when he was wrong. He remembered a comment from an old girlfriend: "I thought you knew it." And he had shrugged. "Well, I didn't know I was wrong." She had looked at him with wide eyes. "Well, you looked so sure of it."

Self-Affirmation is positive thinking. Use Self-Hypnoses to gain a more positive outlook on life. There are a number of Web-Sites where you can find information about these two topics.

Be Friendly

Saturday night John dragged himself out to a bar and club that a band was playing at with a lead singer John knew from years ago. John showed up at this club around ten. The band's first showing was at eleven, so he sat at the bar and ordered a pint. He watched the people around him as he was watching the game on the televisions.

John saw some people dancing to the music that was playing on the stereo. Most of what he saw were kids in their twenties trying to fit in. There were tables by the other bar counter across the dance floor. John couldn't make out what they were saying at the back wall where friends were talking around tables. He held his spot on a stool at the bar where people had to get in close to each other to talk, but he just ordered another pint.

Soon he had to visit the restroom. On his way, he found that the band was setting up, so he stopped to say hi to his friend. His friend gave the expected "Hi, how have you been?" and went back to work on tuning his guitar.

On his way back from the bathroom, John stopped by a few girls. After three girls turned away, he gave it one more shot. Before she could blow him off, the band started playing, so John stuck around to dance with her, or at least by her.

Sunday went by quickly, but Monday John did some research on habits and how they affect people's lives. He found some information to share, so he logged on early to find Tarry and Mike chatting.

Tarry1978: Mike, I told Carle how Kym and Cathie annoyed me and she started to tell me how they annoyed her and everyone heard. I think Jamie agreed, because we kept our distance from those two. I did have to tolerate Carle, but she's just too loud and Jamie knows that.

Mike1991: That's great. I've stayed quiet, but they aren't bothering me as much now. I've been spending more time with Nancy, and some of her friends have joined me with the other group that I have started to bond with.

Tarry1978: Bonding with people seems hard, but some people can bond over the smallest things.

Mike1991: I know, some people are just hanging with me because of how I stood up to Jay. I didn't think I was tough, but some of these people are saying the strangest things.

Anna1983: Mike, don't get arrogant. These people are just looking for someone to follow!

Mike1991: Excuse me!

Anna1983: I mean, most leaders are arrogant, but they use the emotional communication with these people.

Mike1991: I'm not trying to get anything from them. We are just laughing, but I think it's getting boring, so I'll have to come up with a new story.

Anna1983: Just don't get full of yourself.

Alex1986: Mike, don't take that the wrong why, but Anna is right, and so are you. I've had a friend that was quiet until he got attention, but he raved too much and pushed his closest friends away. Now, you can use this attention in a good way, but you need to find more to talk about. How many times did you mention that story in your notes, let alone that post I just read?

Tarry1978: I thought it was funny. There are some girls that are so arrogant that they tell us about something that has happened to them and they think they have to tell it again and again. Mike, you should use this attention you're getting, but find more to talk about and use emotional communication to have a conversation with these people. I hate it when arrogant people just talk at you.

John2010: I was going to wait to talk about arrogant people, but the best way to deal with them is to treat them as your equal. If you want them to pay attention to you, just impress them with something you know or can do better than them. That brings us to habits, because habits are something you're good at.

Anna1983: I used to smoke. That wasn't a good habit.

John2010: I'm glad to hear that you are strong enough to overcome that habit. Smoking made you comfortable, and you liked it when you started. Now, what did you replace it with? Hopefully you found an enjoyable hobby. We did talk about hobbies, but they too are like habits. Habits are things you do every day so you get good at them. If you could start a new habit, what would it be?

Tarry1978: Jamie has the habit of needing something different to do every week. I would like the habit of winning the lottery, so I could give that to her.

Mike1991: Yeah, that would be a great habit, but a costly one most likely.

John2010: Yes, but you all should be looking at these people that you want to change and finding their habits. You can use these habits to control them or to change their ways. Now, Tarry, Jamie is just looking for attention a bit too much and can be inflexible at times. I mean, that's what I see from your posts.

Anna1983: I like how you pointed that out. I think she can be a bit of a brat when she finds something interesting to her...

Tarry1978: Okay, okay. Now, John, why don't you tell us about you!

John2010: I would tell you about my friends, but I don't have any that I would hang out with anymore.

Alex1986: Yeah, I hear you, but why don't you tell us why or what happened with them?

John2010: My last close girlfriend thought I was controlling, judgmental, and loud. You know, arrogant. But she stayed with me for a long time before coming to that conclusion! That was when I thought of changing my ways, because she hurt me and she took all of her friends with her. I never had many friends, though I'm sure there were plenty that would call me a friend. I just wasn't that social. Jen would say that's because I was just a conceited fool.

Tarry1978: So why are we listening to you?

John2010: I've changed...

Anna1983: I was wondering if you had a sociology degree or something. Now we know you've had firsthand experience of being an idiot. Now you want to reestablish yourself by helping us.

Mike1991: Really, that is okay! I need all the help I can get. I'm not social, but John is helping me learn how to be.

John2010: It's not just me. You all are helping each other by having these meetings to help us stick with it. The daily notes are good to keep your goals in sight. I'm just the conduit to help you find greatness.

Tarry1978: Okay, okay, I find all of this helpful and I would never have found it on my own. I would like to hear about John's—our guru—experiences with his friends.

John2010: Let's start at high school. By then I'd developed a reputation for having a short temper. I was too demanding as I communicated, but I wasn't violent, not anymore. I always had to have my way. My friends were mostly sheep, but by my senior year I gathered friends. These friends were in groups that I took part in, but I never felt a part of any group.

Alex1986: You were a loner in high school. I've done that but I try to get over it quickly.

Mike1991: I thought I was a loner, but I think I just had to find myself.

Alex1986: Exactly, I just feel a need to be part of something, so I join in at most places.

Anna1983: I wish I could do that. If I'm not with a friend, I'm lost.

Tarry1978: I'm a loner, but Jamie keeps me actively social enough.

John2010: When I started college I was lonely, but the people there were more welcoming. I found friends in each class, because it wasn't like I was shy. When people see that you have an opinion, they join you. If they agree with it or not, they just want to share their opinions with someone. The best way to find friends is to speak out, but not too loudly.

Tarry1978: One of Jamie's new friend's has an opinion about everything.

Alex1986: I've had a friend like that, but he got too mean for my taste.

Tarry1978: Right, that's what I don't like about this girl. Jamie just thinks she's funny.

John2010: Let this girl know that she is being inappropriate. You should make a list of witty things to say that throw those comments of hers back at her. If you can't just tell her, then show her by acting overly annoyed by it. I said witty, not mean!

Anna1983: This girl has learned that she will get attention with those opinions. I try to ignore people like that.

Mike1991: I wish I could. They won't stop if you ignore them, so I think John is right.

John2010: Thanks for fueling my arrogance. The next few years in college went by too fast, and I did make some good friends. I wasn't the leader of any of these groups, but by the end of college they all thought I should become a lawyer. I always tried to convince the groups that my way was the way to go, and I wasn't using Emotional Communication.

Tarry1978: So you weren't very friendly. Two of the girls that are in the group Jamie has forced me into are like that. They get mad at each other one minute, but the next they are laughing. Another girl keeps telling them to get a room, but I don't think they are that close. They have their own groups that hang out together.

Alex1986: Subgroups that cause conflicts can make the group stronger. I had friends that would stick with a group because of the conflicts. Tarry, it sounds like you like to speak your mind. These new friends may be good for you to start expressing yourself more with. Don't be afraid to speak your opinions, even if you don't think one of these girls won't like it.

Anna1983: It's okay to be opinionated, but don't get arrogant like that girl you don't like. John did say to let her know that how she is acting is inappropriate, so show her how to do it in an acceptable manner.

John2010: Yes, and use emotional communication. Tonight I hope you all understand that it's okay to speak out; just be considerate. This week look for your friends' habits and as you write them down, find your own habits and write them down.

John logged out, leaving this group chatting about how to express themselves with emotional communication. They came to the conclusion that they should start off with a joke, and then state that they understand that some people don't agree with what they're saying but...

As John was writing the e-mails to this group, he thought that he should include his insights on a story he read to tonight's e-mails.

I was reading a paper about how just hearing or reading an experience can affect you physically. Have you talked with a friend about a tragedy that has happened to them and felt upset yourself? I'm sure you have, but these things can affect your life more than you realize.

How often has your' eating habits changed after hearing something that you could feel in your stomach. Just an example of how hearing or reading about traumatic experiences can change your' life.

Family Matters

Tuesday came and went with John going about his normal routine, but Wednesday came quickly and he reviewed Monday's posts. John thought of events in his life that might be worth sharing, but he didn't find many actual encounters.

John did take notes of life-changing events from his life, but he didn't see any specific events. John saw how he had evolved and looked on-line for short stories to use that would affect the changes that he had found in his life.

John logged on to the blog and found Amy and Sledge chatting about Amy's post. To his surprise he found that Alex had joined them again tonight.

Amy1979: I know, but I just want Jim to understand that he doesn't need to do that.

Sledge1984: Maybe he does it for himself, not for you... From what I've read, he is the quiet type and he may be doing things for you to make him feel better, not you. I don't want to say that all quiet people are like this, but people do things that make them feel good. Quiet people may keep these things to themselves better.

Amy1979: Jim was acting different, but then he started to go out to that bar. Now he's just going out once a week, but he is getting back to just sitting around the house.

Sledge1984: Isn't that what you want him to do?

Alex1986: I think she is just worried about him doing nothing and getting into mischief.

Amy1979: Well, I'm doing something. That hobby I've started has kept me busy and he just reads the newspaper.

John2010: Maybe that's his hobby and the things he does for you make him feel like he has accomplished something. Didn't I suggest that you find a hobby that you can do together? Now, don't stop your hobby and don't stop him from reading the newspaper. You are getting something out of your hobby that he can't see, as I'm sure he is getting something out of reading the paper that you can't see. Maybe you should ask him what news he is reading about in the paper.

Amy1979: I get enough news at dinner on TV.

Alex1986: Well, you may find something that he is reading interesting.

John2010: Okay, ask Jim to help you or do something that you would like him to do, so he doesn't feel he has to find something to do for you. Use emotional communication when asking him for anything. Ask him, "Why don't you help me…?" and don't give lists. You could offer to help him with something he likes doing even if he doesn't need it. Everybody likes being shown interest and helped with things that they enjoy doing.

Rick1982: Right. I was helping my wife to get what she was working on done faster and I found that we connected. She started talking about someone at work and she really opened up when I started asking questions about this person. Then I brought up some things that I've been meaning to talk to her about.

Sledge1984: Yeah, Barb needs to keep her mouth busy when her hands are busy. I used to think this was annoying, but now I've learned to listen and to lead Barb into talking about what I wanted to talk to her about.

John2010: This week I wanted to talk about habits, but I thought I should tell you what they are first and over this week you can find your habits and your friends' habits.

John copied and pasted the posts about habits from Monday's meeting, and he added the group's questions and his answers. He added the comments that the subjects made from the friends relations group also. John told tonight's group that he was asked about his life, and posted the vague comments that he made to the group on Monday.

John2010: I thought of life-changing experiences to share with them next time. I had time to prepare some family-changing events that I thought I should share with you all. I thought that you may get an idea of how or what to change with your families.

When I was younger I found that it was easy for me not to use emotional communication with my family, and I would expect things to be, to happen, and I wouldn't show any appreciation. My sister wouldn't like to spend time with me and we grew apart. My father got tired of me and just got into the "you can do it for yourself" mode.

I have had fights with my sister when I was young. We would fight over common things, but she did something that really upset me, and she didn't even know it. Over the years I learned to forgive her, and that changed how I acted toward her and she noticed it if just in her subconscious. I started to always say that I'm sorry for the littlest troubles, so that she doesn't feel so put out.

John2010: The moral of these two experiences are, don't take family for granted, and it's easier to forgive than hold a grudge against a family member.

Rick1982: I hear you, John. Joe and I have had some fights that we held for a long time. Recently I haven't been thinking about them, so I missed Joe. That's why I've been trying a new way to talk with him, but those fights have come back into my mind. I should learn to get over it.

Amy1979: Yeah, if you can forgive and forget, then it won't hold you back.

Sledge1984: Hold you back from what?

John2010: Holding a grudge against anyone makes it harder to be around them. Forgiveness makes life easier. Now, I'm not saying to forgive everyone for everything. Those who you love and people that you have no choice but to make a part of your life, it is relieving after you have forgiven them.

Amy1979: Okay, I see that, but what if you can't stop thinking about it? Or every time you see that person, the memories come back?

John2010: Make new memories. When you see that person, think of future events with them. Use the jar of life to find those little things that you like about them.

Alex1986: I was taking a closer look at the jar about my sister and I found something. When I saw her next I was going into that defense posture, because her friend was with her. I remembered to smile and look welcoming when I saw them. I asked what they were up to, and I asked her if she was still doing that, and I talked with her and her friend.

Sledge1984: Oh, that one girl was coming on to you. I like how you described your sister's snake eyes, and her friend just fell away. ☺

Amy1979: Yeah, but you did start a conversation with your sister and her two friends. So now you can become more of a part of her life. I couldn't laugh and talk with Jim's friends. I've seen how he reacts when I talk to other men, innocently. He draws back, but I can see that he doesn't like it.

Alex1986: Well, he thinks you're his, and you should be glad he shies away. I used to have a friend who was possessive and he got upset when a guy said more than hi to his girl. Now, he didn't get violent, but he was crushed when she broke it off. I think Jim is a lot more emotional than you see.

Amy1979: Oh, I am noticing that his emotions change more than I thought. I know that everybody has emotions, but his are happy, sad, and angry. Now I've been looking closer, and even his eyes change, if only just the slightest bit.

John2010: Yes, Alex, good story. Family members can be too possessive of each other. Amy, that's good that you are noticing the slightest changes in Jim's face. I hope you all are seeing these changes. That is how you read people and know what's coming next before it happens.

Rick1982: Right, I thought I could read my wife good, but then I started to look for the things in her jar, and I can see how blind I was. I see that there is more to her now.

Sledge1984: I'm seeing more of my wife's family and they try too hard to be friendly with everyone. It's not just her father, but he is the best at it. I mean, he can befriend anyone fast. Much like you, Alex!

Alex1986: Well, it's a habit. I am just more comfortable when I have a friend. When I join a new group I tend to attach to someone in it. I don't always make the best choice of who I attach to.

Amy1979: I never join new groups unless one of my friends is a part of the group. I can't talk to strangers unless they start talking with me first, and even then I'm not forthcoming.

John2010: Well, there you go. Alex has a habit of befriending strangers and Amy has a habit of not being forthcoming with strangers. Now I would like you all to find your habits and see why you have them. Alex already told us why he has a habit of befriending strangers, but why does Amy have trouble with that? Don't just say that she's not outgoing, but ask why she's not. Now, Amy, look into your jar of life through your own life. You may have learned not to be forthcoming because of something that has happened in your past. Just finding that thing may help you to be more outgoing, because it doesn't concern your life now.

Amy1979: I was just taught to beware of strangers.

John2010: That is good for children to learn and when you are out on a strange street. When you are with like-minded people that you aren't affiliated with, but as a group, you should be able to express yourself. Habits are something you're good at and enjoy, but habits can hold you back. That is why you need to find what originated them in your life. Once you have found what has formed your habits, you can create new habits.

Rick1982: Okay, so habits are more like everything we enjoy doing, but bad habits are what we have learned to do to help cope. Now you want us to find these good habits and bad habits to help us see how to change ourselves.

Alex1986: I think you've caught on to what John is really having us change.

John2010: I want you to find these habits in the people that you are trying to change also. Once you've found how to affect your wife's habits, Rick, you can change her at will.

Amy1979: Oh, that's bad, but I can see how to use habits to change people.

Sledge1984: You would, you see how you can be more controlling. Oh, and you don't like strangers, because you can't control them.

John2010: Amy, I'm sure that Sledge didn't mean to be so blunt, but let's sign off on that. Next week I hope to hear how habits control your families' lives and how to use them to cause great change.

John logged off, leaving his subjects chatting at each other. He read through the weekly posts and was happy to see how long they'd gotten. Alex left a short post with this group also that was about how he has missed spending time with one of his sisters. John left specific comments in the e-mails, but he could relate with Alex's post and added an experience that he'd had with his sister. John added that story to each e-mail to be more open and he could see how the others would relate it to something in their lives.

My sister and I weren't close through high school, but after she graduated from college I hoped to spend time with her. She did spend a few years at the house after college, but she stayed in her room mostly. When she would come down to watch TV she wouldn't like me to be in the room.

I just turned her off, I wish I hadn't, I believe that communication was at fault. I did join her at times, but they didn't last. I thought she was pushing me away. If I listened more and saw how she would express herself we may have been closer.

John thought he should share the story about how just hearing about a tragedy can affect you.

Yes, feeling for someone you love is important, but feeling too much can be tragic. When you hear about something horrific that has happened to them, you can feel the pain in your mind and body. Hearing about it, reading about it, talking about it, thinking about it, dwelling on it can hurt you as much as it would, happening to you.

Habits at Work

John looked on-line for more information to share with his subjects about work relations and habits. He mostly found information about inappropriate relations at work. John did find a story about a man who got ahead at a job where he was overlooked by most of his coworkers. He thought of sharing it with them as his own, but John put together some information about habits. He didn't think he was ready with any new information, but he thought that all habits were relevant.

As John logged on, he found that the subjects had a list of their habits in the week's post. Most of them had accounts of how these habits affected their day at work. John took more time reading the posts to put together what he wanted to talk to these subjects about.

Jill1959: I was looking at my habits and found things that I've done for years, but I don't actually think that I'm good at them. It took a while but I was writing them all down and then separating them by good and bad. I found that I'm better at some of the bad habits.

Sally1974: What makes them bad? I found some habits that you may think are bad, but I found that they make me feel good.

Bill4267: That's why they are so addictive, but John said to find out why you do them. I found out why they feel good, and mostly it's the accomplishment that feels good. Now, I'm not talking about habits that may hurt you like substance abuse or any rapid hand movements.

Jill1959: I have that habit of typing fast and my hands are hurting. Really I have noticed that when I take my time typing, my hands don't hurt as much. I have hot and cold hand raps that work good. Anyway, I see that the accomplishment of a task is uplifting or reassuring.

Timmy1982: I just remembered reading that if you picture a task done, then you don't put it off, you get it done. My everyday habits that are just work, this week I have been picturing the end of the day coming faster if I just get the work done. In that e-mail John sent me, he pointed out that after I have that meeting with those two men, I would feel better, or as if I've accomplished what I wanted.

Bill4267: That's right. After you have accomplished a task, you feel good no matter how small it is, and the more challenging it is, the better you feel.

Jill1959: After I have struggled with getting something done, I feel better. I just think I feel so good because my struggle is over. I get the same feeling when I'm working on a doll or a presentation.

Timmy1982: Yes, but are these things habits?

Bill4267: Only if you do them often enough.

John2010: I've read all of your habits and how you use them. Timmy, I'm glad to hear that you are accomplishing more and feeling good about it before it's done. If any of you aren't understanding what Timmy is doing, then you just need a better imagination. Really you need to see it done in your mind and feel it as being accomplished. Bill, I'm glad you pointed out that accomplishments feel good.

Sally1974: Okay, so habits are everyday accomplishments that we are good at because they feel good.

Timmy1982: I think that we get good at habits because we do them every day. If they feel good, then that's a bonus.

John2010: Most people do what makes them feel good. If at work you have something to do that doesn't feel good, then just think of how good it will feel after it has been done. Now, in today's posts I see that some of you are focused on the bad things that happen. The weekly posts should be focused on the positive things, because the bad things are easy to remember.

Sally1974: I thought we were picking apart our lives to find the bad and good things that make us.

John2010: That's right, with the jar of life, but now we want to find how to make bad habits good. We can use them to help shape your life and the people around you. We listed our habits, and most of you have divided them from good habits and bad habits. I'm glad to see that a few of you even listed how they make you feel.

Jill1959: Right, I was reading that and I looked at my habits again. Then Bill pointed out how it feels to accomplish them. I looked at one habit that I have to do at work, but I don't like it and thought, if I just would look forward to the completion of it, I would feel better.

Sally1974: There are a number of things I don't enjoy at work, but I've gotten rather good at getting them done. I have learned to just get them done, but I should look forward to having them done.

John2010: Good, it is important to look forward to how good it feels to finish something that you don't like doing. Now let's discus your coworkers' habits and how we can change them to change how these coworkers see us.

Sally1974: There is a girl at work who has a habit of always having something to complain about.

Timmy1982: There was a man at work who had that habit. I used that emotional communication on him, and I let him know how it made me feel seeing him always complaining about his life.

Sally1974: If I do that, this girl will complain about me.

Timmy1982: Well, that sounds like you're scared to upset this girl, which gives you a good reason to talk to her. Now, I didn't just go up to this guy and tell him that it upsets me to see him complain about his life. I first talked to him about what he was complaining about and showed him that I could relate, but then I told him that it brought me down to see him complain. Then another guy who was in the break room pointed out that we do have people in the building to complain to or talk to for support.

Bill4267: I saw therapists at work once, and they were helpful, but it got redundant, so I stopped seeing them.

Jill1959: Well, I saw someone after I lost my husband, I think talking with my friends was better than talking with a stranger.

John2010: Now therapy is good, it can help you see your life in a different way. Timmy is right, you use emotional communication to affect someone's habits. You can let them know that what they are doing is having a negative effect on you or someone else. If they start a habit that you like, just complimenting someone on it can have the effect of them doing it more often. If someone feels that they are having an effect on someone it will make them think. The idea is to make them think how you want them to.

Sally1974: I don't like the idea of manipulating thoughts.

Timmy1982: TV does it, our government does it, but there is too much mind manipulation out there. I've always wanted to learn how to use it. Really, everybody does it, even if they don't know it. One of my girlfriends had a book about psychic self-defense, and it's scary out there.

Bill4267: Please don't talk about psychics. One of my ex-wives was into the paranormal, and it ruined us.

Jill1959: Okay, but, Sally, I don't blame you for not liking manipulative people. Emotional communication is the first step to manipulation, and I think fallowing people's habits just helps us use it.

Timmy1982: Right. Learning our coworkers' jars of life was the first step. Now we are finding their habits, so that we can see how we can change them to make a big difference in our lives.

Bill4267: Well, you've convinced me that if we change someone's habits, it will have a big effect on their lives. My first wife had a friend that she always did something with, but they stopped and that changed her drastically. I didn't realize it until now, but that may have been what she lost. She was saying…

John2010: Okay, Bill, good example, but this is the work relations group, and I'd like to see how habits affect the work environment. I see that most of you have listed things that have become habits, because of your job. These habits make you good at your job. Some of you have complaints about these habits, so who can tell me how to make these tasks less bothersome?

Jill1959: Think of them being finished.

Sally1974: Yeah, imagine the feeling you'll have after accomplishing them.

John2010: If you have a strong enough imagination, then you won't be able to put those tasks off.

Timmy1982: Are the things we do at work habits?

Bill4267: Only if you do them enough. This tactic should work with just about everything.

John2010: Yes, we are discussing habits, because they are the things you do every day, and if you think of the everyday tasks differently than the major things that you want to change in your lives will come easier. Starting a habit with one of your coworkers can be easy. Sally, that girl that complains a lot may just need something ells to do. Jill, when you shared your hobby with some coworkers, didn't they change how they looked at you?

Jill1959: Oh, now they have the habit of smiling when they see me. I think that's because they are connecting me to the dolls and the fun we had. When you first told us to pay more attention to people's expressions, I didn't like what I was seeing. I think I had learned not to see it, or to look past expressions like that, but now I've learned to see them and I see how they've changed.

Sally1974: That's great, Jill. I have seen some changes in how I'm looked upon, but I think a lot of them still think I'm ditsy.

John2010: Don't think you know what they are thinking of you; just see what they show you. Now, thinking that someone is looking down on you will just drain your confidence. If you remember, a few weeks ago I told you about the best way to build confidence is with positive reinforcement, by leaving notes that you'll see a number of times a day.

Timmy1982: Right, I tried that and it really works. At work I took a 3-by-5 card and wrote, "BE PROUD!" When I see that, I think of things I'm proud about. That puts a smile on my face.

Jill1959: I guess different things work, but I already have notes and lists. At the top of the lists, I have started to write a comment that reflects how I want to feel that day, and I think it's making a difference.

Bill4267: I didn't think this idea was for me, but now that I think about it, if I had a note on my desk that told me to be confident, it would just get annoying.

John2010: Bill, it's the annoying things that you remember and that make the difference. You all should have found out what annoys you the most. If you can activate that feeling, then use it to help activate your memory. Or you can do it the hard way and relate what you have to remember to something you can't forget. Use a memory door, when you open it you see an image of what you have attached the thing you need to remember to. It's easier to remember something when you attach a feeling to it. Just some advice, but I'm glad you can see how hearing about bad experiences affects you. I have a story on that topic that will be attached to your e-mails, so let's sign off with that.

John just shook his head, thinking, *If I tell them now, what will I have for them next week?*

John was happy with tonight's group and rereads their weekly posts. He added a number of specific comments to the e-mails he sent to each subject. John thought that these subjects had absorbed his idea and were using it in their own way. He thought Bill was the least open to change, but John saw in the weekly posts how Bill had used the little things to change people at work.

Bill had pointed out how it had gotten annoying that more people were talking to him at work. He had noticed that the few men that he was trying to gain attention from were seeing him in a better light. Bill wrote that he was surprised that, now that he had gained some annoying acquaintances at work, he had also gained the attention from some of his managers.

Timmy was raving about the attention he was getting from the head manager of a totally different department. He wrote that his boss was questioning his motives more than anything, but he was getting the attention he was hoping for from him.

Friendly Habits

Over the weekend, John stayed in, and did more research on habits. He found some family habits and roommate habits. From Friday's group and what John found on-line, he put some notes together to share with the friends group.

Monday came fast, and John worked on compiling the information from this blog he had started into a book. He thought he had what he wanted to share with tonight's group, but like on Friday he knew that they would have their own topics.

On Friday John sent a page about harassing fellow workers. His last comment was to be careful with a joke at work, because at work not everyone is like-minded.

John logged on to the blog and found Anna and Mike chatting about their week.

Anna1983: I used emotional communication with Patty's friend Sue and I was finding out some changes that Patty is going through at work. I think I sounded too interested, because she told me to ask Patty as she was coming back. I took a breath and, well, Patty just didn't want to talk about work, so I clammed up as they talked for a bit.

Mike1991: I do that also. When I'm talking and get interrupted, it takes a while to get back into the conversation. I don't know, but I just don't have the nerve to interrupt, but when I have something to say I can go on and on.

Anna1983: Yeah, but Patty is a good friend because she is a good communicator and she's patient. That's what I like about this group. John is actually teaching us how to communicate. I know that listening is a big part of communication, but John told us what to look for and how to listen.

Mike1991: I am seeing more in my friends' attitudes when they talk, so I know how to respond. Like some of these new friends are genuinely concerned or are enjoying my company. The other half are looking to the sky half the time and want to move on. I am learning when to ask questions or make a new opinion about something they are into.

Anna1983: I am learning to carry a conversation too. When I was with a different group, I could see that they were losing interest in what one guy was talking about. I actually offered my input on it and started a joke, but then people looked at me to continue. I was like, ah, but I started to tell them about Patty and when she said...

Alex1986: When I was reading your post I was thinking Anna has evolved out of her cocoon. I mean, you were talking about Patty, who you've been using as a crutch, but she wasn't there.

Anna1983: Very funny, Alex.

John2010: I was reading the lists of your friends' habits, and I looked at the habits you've listed for yourselves, and saw that most of you have the same habits as your friends. A friend that you have a habit to share with can become a better friend. The subgroups are formed by sharing habits. Mike, I see that you don't like some of the habits of your new friends. You can try to change them by using emotional communication and letting them know. You can find a habit that you share and use that to help the relationship grow in a different direction. Now you know how to change someone by using emotional communication with them and their closest friends. Tonight let's chat about habits and changing them.

Tarry1978: Oh, I used emotional communication and changed how Jamie sees the new group she found. Now she's tired of them, but we will still keep in touch with some of them. She can change overnight…

Mike1991: Right, some of my new friends change day by day. I just have to say the right thing to the right person. Oh, and it may not seem to be the good thing, but to have the effect that you are looking for, you sometimes need to make a point. Yes, that does backfire, but I think I explained myself to Nancy.

Anna1983: I don't. She is probably questioning her whole relationship with you.

John2010: Now, Mike, what I would do to help Nancy forget what you did is to spend time with her doing those habits and hobby's you both enjoy. Show her that there is more to you than how you treated her friend. I do see why you did that, and it looks like the outcome is benefitting your agenda.

Anna1983: I don't like talk like that, because it sounds as if you're trying to take advantage of your friends. I know that we are learning to read them to get closer, but when you use what you learned like that, it doesn't feel right.

Alex1986: I was reading Mike's post and he isn't being mean, but misleading them can make them feel as bad. I had a friend who would be misleading and then laugh about it. Now, that was bad. Mike is using what he learned from the lists he made about his new friends and is stepping up. I don't see anything that is genuinely wrong about it. As I mentioned in my post, Kim and I have talked and she started acting weird, so I told her, "Ah, Kim, I am just trying to make this good between us so Jessie stops pushing me away..."

Tarry1978: Right, you need to be careful with people that love you. I got a strange look from Jamie when I started showing too much interest in something, because she knows me. All I'm saying is when you act different with someone that knows how you normally act, you need to keep some habits.

John2010: Good point, your closest friends are so close because of your habits and hobbies. If you're close with someone because you enjoy talking with them, what happens when they change what they talk about? That is a simple example, but change makes people uncomfortable, so you need to be aware of how these actions affect those you are closest to.

Anna1983: That's right. Mike, when you are just learning about new friends like Nancy, you need to show her the real you, because she doesn't know any other you.

Mike1991: Okay, I get it. With Nancy and her friends I should show the me I want her to like. The other group of friends that I feel I can call my friends now I have to act like I'm more on, if you know what I mean.

Alex1986: I know exactly what you mean. I had a small mishap with my girlfriend once, and I was thinking about it. I wasn't myself all weekend at the beach. One of the guys kept asking what was wrong and finally I said, "I'm just not on this week." and he asked, "Where's the switch?" What I'm saying is that if I was home with my friends they wouldn't have known anything was wrong.

Tarry1978: I guess that guy just knows you better.

Alex1986: Not really. What I mean is that I'm not myself with those guys. I always have to be on or they think something's wrong.

Anna1983: There was something wrong. You had a fight with your girlfriend.

Alex1986: No, I was just getting tired of her and let that out.

Tarry1978: Oh, I think Jamie is getting tired of me…

Alex1986: Even after you got her away from those new friends of hers?

Tarry1978: Well, I think she went out and got those new friends because she's getting bored with me.

John2010: That's what you get for thinking…

Mike1991: I think what John is getting at is that you should take your friends at their word and not to think too much into it.

Tarry1978: Yeah, thinking too much always causes problems…

Alex1986: I know what you mean. One of my girlfriends was running her mind crazy, but it was like two people with her. One minute she was fine, but the next she would almost cry. I thought I should end it with her, but I didn't want to see her hurt. Now I can see she is overdramatic to gain attention and I can see it coming.

Mike1991: Is this Kim?

Alex1986: Anyway, I listed that as a habit. Now, I did come to this blog looking for help with my girlfriend and her friends. I think I am getting too close to them now. I think Jessie doesn't like it. At first I knew that she may have a problem, so I approached them as a group. That did work out, but then Carle trapped me alone and we started talking. I mean, she did help me get in better with Jessie's parents, but we talked too long. After she fell into my arms I knew we were too close.

Mike1991: Oh. When I read that Jessie was right there looking down on you, I couldn't stop laughing.

Anna1983: I was reading your post and thought you were trying to get with all of these girls. I thought again and what you did was just talking and it would have been okay if these girls were your sisters, but a girl can get overemotional when she talks to a man in that way.

Mike1991: John, you should have told Alex to be careful when using emotional communication.

John2010: Alex, be careful. Now, from your posts I can see that you don't mean any misgivings toward these girls. I'm not sure that I could help you with how to deal with Jessie, but to spend time with her doing the things she loves. Share the habits and hobbies that you both enjoy. Let her know why you love her and use emotional communication to let her know about your actions that may have upset her. The reason most people get upset is that they don't know the whole truth, and feed the half-truths with misgivings.

Tarry1978: That's deep, John, and it's true. When I don't understand what's happening, I fear the worst. I guess that's why you told us not to think too much into our friends' misgivings until we are sure of what they are.

John2010: That's right. Now, habits are things people enjoy doing. When someone is enjoying a habit, their emotions change, so you can change people's feelings by changing a habit. How do you encourage a habit? By using emotional communication to bend the person's views. The best way to change a habit of a person is by changing how a friend or family member of this person views this habit. Then you have them encourage this person to change.

Alex1986: I have changed my relationship with Jessie's family by using Carle to get closer to them. I'm glad that you had us find these habits to use, because it showed me how to talk with Jessie's father. In the post I told you all how I got closer with him by talking about Jessie and finding what he wished would change about her. I told him that I'd like to see some of those changes and he said that he has learned to keep a distance from some subjects. Now that I see what he would like to see, I can change them to gain a different perspective from him.

Mike1991: Alex, do you want to marry this girl or something?

Alex1986: Not this year, but if I play my cards right, she will want and be expecting me to ask her. Not too long from now because…

Anna1983: That's great, Alex, you should take to heart what John has suggested and be open with her.

John2010: Yes... Well, I hope you all have taken advantage of my suggestions over these eight weeks, because I don't have much more for you. You are all more than welcome to use this blog page to talk with each other, but this will be my last week. I may tune in every now and then, though.

Anna1983: What about me? My problems have just started...

John2010: I think we have conquered your biggest problem. Just don't crawl back into that cocoon. I will be sending reply's to each of the posts tonight and you are all welcome to join us on Wednesday. I hope you all do well in all of your expeditions...

John left them chatting about how mean he was for leaving them. John logged off and rereads the posts and gave good reviews and suggestions in the replies to each of them.

Family Habits

John was writing his book all day Tuesday. On Wednesday he rereads what he had written and was tempted to copy and paste each of the weekly posts, but he thought better. Wednesday night came fast, but John logged on to the blog early. He didn't want tonight's group to be about how he was leaving. He found that he wasn't the first one there. Amy was raving to Rick about how Jim and she had started a new date night.

Amy1979: Jim is reading the book also. I like that we are reading together after dinner. Jim used to just stick his nose in the newspaper after dinner.

Rick1982: So he's doing the same thing...

Amy1979: No, we talk about each chapter. On Saturday evenings we get together with the book club and we talk about the books. I am impressed with how Jim opened up at the first meeting.

Rick1982: Well, I guess he wanted to be sure they were reading books that he would enjoy.

Amy1979: He was rolling his eyes at one of the subgroups that is into fantasy, but he was talking with the scientists.

Rick1982: There are scientists in this club?

Amy1979: Well, a science teacher and a researcher who got the nickname The Scientists.

Rick1982: That's good, he found new friends. My wife has opened up some more with me, but Crista doesn't like going out after work. She works most weekends and I work all week, so we have been talking more at dinner and after dinner. When Crista watches her entertainment news, I sit there with the newspaper, but at commercials we talk.

Amy1979: That's what we used to do after dinner, minus the talking. Now we are talking about the book and I've found it to be easier to talk about other things too. I asked Jim what he was talking to the scientists about, and then I asked if he talked to people at work like that...

John2010: That's great, Amy, getting Jim to open up to you and finding other people to talk to can help him at work. Rick, it is good that you have found a time to talk with your wife. As you talk with Crista you can find other things to talk about and find new interests. That is what I hope we are all after, finding out more about our family to spend more time with them.

Sledge1984: Yes, I have enjoyed the more time that I've spent with my wife and her family now more than I could have imagined. I mean, I used to fear going to Barb's family's house, but now that I've looked into her family more, I have fun.

Rick1982: Oh, I know what you mean. I haven't seen Crista's family recently, but I've looked into their jars and found new things. I can't wait to see them again to use my emotional communication skills with them. At work I've used these skills and made friends that I wouldn't have if I didn't learn to look deeper.

John2010: That's great. It sounds like you have all benefited from these meetings. I came early tonight and was pleased to find that you're all looking forward to talking about habits. I invited people from the friends group to join us tonight. I would like to ask them not to share the surprise, because I don't want to have it hovering over tonight's meeting.

Alex1986: Okay, John! I can relate with you guys. I have gotten closer to Jessie's family by looking into their jars of life. I used one of Jessie's friends to help approach her parents, but to do this I may have gotten too close or emotional with her. I called Jessie today and we talked and we are getting together tomorrow to talk more. The tone I got from her was that she thinks I have something to confess. I'm afraid she won't let me start by leading her into being open-hearted, into what I want to say.

Amy1979: I know how annoying it is when someone has tunnel vision and just hears what they want to. That is why you start with emotional communication, and you should be good at it from what I've read from you. Starting with a story that shows that you can relate to the situation is good emotional communication. This conversation you're having already started, so to put her at ease I would start with what you've already told her.

Alex1986: Right, right, John told us on Monday that what upsets most people is when the person doesn't know the whole story. So, I should make sure she understands what I meant to say to her on the phone the other day, first.

Sledge1984: Is that what you didn't want him to tell us? Because I know the whole story, and I'm still upset. Really,

I get that if someone doesn't know the whole truth, they usually jump to the worst conclusions. Why is that?

Rick1982: I think that's just the way of life. The first thing people see is the worst of each other.

John2010: That's a defense mechanism or the effect of being taken advantage of.

Anna1983: Nobody likes being taken for a fool. Like your girlfriend, Alex, I would expect the worst after that conversation you had with her. When I read today's short post from you, I had my hand to my mouth. I hope you said more to her than you told us, but I think you should first apologize for that phone call.

Alex1986: I was wondering when you were going to chime in. That is a good suggestion. I should apologize for being so brief. Then I can relate to her confusion with a short story about my confusion because of a blunt conversation I had. A blunt transfer is worse than a brief transfer.

Amy1979: Aren't they the same thing?

Alex1986: Well, I can tell it as if my experience was worse.

John2010: Okay, now your lists of habits, I see that most of you want to change your families' habits. You have expanded the jar of life with these habits, so you can see how important they are. You can use the more important habits to get closer to the subject and promote or discourage a minor habit. These minor habits can be called fads that won't last unless you let them. These habits can change someone's outlook to a subject that they or you are dealing with at the moment.

Amy1979: Jim has the habit, that when he gets home from work he first uses the toilet, and then he lounges out in his chair, before saying hi to me. I guess that is okay. He has to clear his mind after work.

John2010: Amy, weren't you going to use notes to promote his confidence?

Amy1979: That was Rick who was doing that.

Rick1982: I did that to promote my confidence. My wife adds things to do.

Sledge1984: Yeah, and it works. I use that note program on my PC and I see it first thing and then throughout the day. I'm not one for keeping a schedule, but I've been adding things that need to get done to it.

John2010: Amy, I have a paper at the sink in my bathroom that I look at every time I use it, so I keep a few things in my mind. You can let Jim know that you are thinking of him, and give him confidence.

Amy1979: He won't read it. He probably won't even use the sink.

John2010: You can pin it up over the toilet so he has no choice but to read it.

Sledge1984: I have no choice but to look at my computer screen most of the day. That's why I started leaving on-screen notes.

Rick1982: The first thing is to have in big red letters "RINSE HANDS." It's better than nothing. Oh, then have confidence-building words.

Sledge1984: Yeah, then tell him what to do.

Anna1983: Rinse hands is good, but I was thinking, what will that help? The soap is right there. It will keep it in mind, and you are right, it's better than nothing.

Alex1986: My sister has the habit of being too clean... But at least she keeps the house clean.

John2010: Yes, that is what these notes are for! To keep your mind on track. These notes are a way for you or anybody to start a habit, but they should know why or what the note is for. If you tell a family member or a loved one that you are leaving notes to help, they will be more open to it.

Sledge1984: I don't think that will work. If I tell Andy what I'm doing, he will just do the opposite thing and laugh.

Amy1979: Have you ever heard of reverse psychology? Well, I'm sure you have, but be careful, because he may come back and say, I thought you said...

Rick1982: Reverse psychology may be good with children, but I don't know how good it is with someone that you want to trust you.

John2010: You use emotional communication with a lie to manipulate them to act in a different way. Emotional communication isn't just used to get closer to someone. It can be used to discourage someone from acting or doing something that you don't like. If someone is doing something that you don't like, you can remind them of something that influences their life. This will make them stop and think. Use their jar of life to find this thing that you use to influence them.

Anna1983: I started reading this and didn't like it, or how it sounded, but by the end I could really see how wording can make the difference. I know that "lying to manipulate" means the same thing as "influencing them." They just give me a different feeling.

Amy1979: Not always, but I can see that overly influencing someone can seem to be lying to them. You are right, it maters how and what you say with emotional communication. I was talking to an old friend the other day using emotional communication and I could see how I was dumbing my words down for her.

Sledge1984: Oh yeah, that has become a habit for me when I speak to my wife's brother. I don't know if that's a good habit or a bad one.

John2010: It's a good one. You should know how to simplify what you're talking about with people that don't know. Most people don't know what you talk about. That is why we form groups that know, so we feel comfortable. Now, I feel that I have shared all that I know on this topic, so this will be my last week with you all here. I will be here on Friday for the work group that you are all welcome.

Amy1979: What? I mean, I have learned a lot from you over these past weeks, but I need more help.

Anna1983: I know what you mean. I'm coming on Friday to see if I can get more people to stick with this group.

Rick1982: John, where are you going?

John2010: I just won't be here! I may check in on you guys, but Friday will be my last scheduled time. And if you are here on Friday, please let me, tell them that it will be my last day.

John logged off with the subjects chatting about why he was leaving them and who would be continuing the groups. John rereads the weekly posts and replied to them, giving more advice or suggestions than usual.

Sledge's post had a lot of details about his brother-in-law. Sledge was saying how he was thinking of setting his sister up with him to see what happened. Rick felt that he had gained new trust with his wife. She seemed more open to sharing the events from work and her life. Amy was happy that she was spending more quality time with Jim.

Work Confusions

Friday came quickly and John logged into the blog to find his subjects chatting with excitement.

Bill4267: Timmy, I have read your post and you say that because you have gained friends that you weren't expecting, and I'm glad to hear that your boss is giving you the attention you were looking for.

Timmy1982: Yes, this past week he talked to the head of the department that the guys I have been meeting with are at. My manager is giving me more work now with the relations department we work with and I am hoping I can get a raise, but I'm just getting more work now.

Bill4267: The relations department? That sounds like you will use these skills that John is showing us, with that work.

Timmy1982: I read the people in that office differently. It was like I was seeing more. I mean, I read every expression, but I knew that each expression was just part of how they felt. One girl was upset or annoyed with something or someone, but when I was working with her I could see how she changed and got to work.

Bill4267: I hate that, I put up my defenses or act cautious, and the person changes in an instant or they look fine like everything is okay, but a second later they're in my face about something.

Sally1974: That's great, you guys are being more social. When a boss sees that you're social, he thinks he can trust you to act good with others. Having a good social network helps in all parts of life.

Bill4267: I heard that somewhere, but I never got it. I think it was my first wife. Now I can see the different networks and how they interlink. I still think it is too much of a bother...

Sally1974: Bill, I've seen people that are social just because it makes them look normal. I mean, you don't want to be thought of the quiet guy who sits alone.

Bill4267: Well, I don't see myself as a quiet guy, but now sometimes I get worn out from talking too much.

Jill1959: That's funny, I get tired from talking too much now, but I used to be able to talk all day.

Sally1974: I have talked to my friends forever about nothing, but last Saturday I went out with two friends. When we were talking at lunch, I thought that I should try to use some emotional communication with them. I thought that there wasn't much to find out, but Rebecca opened up to me when Sue was away. Sue returned and she was wild-eyed as I told her what Rebecca had just said.

Timmy1982: Did you ask Rebecca if it was okay to tell her?

Sally1974: Of course! Oh, you know that guy from work, we went out for a drink and he opened up to me about a past relationship that didn't end well.

Mike1991: Sally, I read your post, and that date interests me, because I am making new friends at school and I am interested in getting to know Nancy. The other day a different girl asked me out with her friends, which is a subgroup within this other group of new friends I have. I told her sure, with a look at her friends, meaning that we could all go do something. If what you wrote is what happened with that guy, then I could use some help. How did you keep it so you didn't get too close? When I use emotional communication, I always get too close. This one guy actually said, "You aren't going gay on me, Mike?"

Sally1974: That is funny, but yes, using emotional communication can lead to deep conversations. I'll read your post and get back to you.

John2010: Just a little emotional communication can change your world. Now, Bill and Timmy, I see you're being looked at with a whole new light. It looks like you are getting what you asked for, so be careful. Sally, it looks like you've found more than you were looking for, but that guy at work seems kosher; just make sure his story is true. Jill, you are making more friends at work that aren't just interested in your doll club. These girls seem genuine.

Jill1959: Yes, I do get that feeling and I wouldn't have found them if I didn't start talking with the other girls. More people at work are looking to me for help and less like a burden.

Mike1991: Sally, John's right. I have some other friends that tell stories about the lies they've told girls just to get them in bed…

Anna1983: Sally, Mike may be right. It may have not been your emotional communication and intuitiveness that got that story out of him. I started to read about how you got your friend to open up, but then you stopped.

Sally1974: I just didn't feel right sharing all the info. Mike, when you talk it does matter how you express yourself and with what tense you used. If you used "we," with a look around the room, that means you and everyone else, but if you use "we," with a look in her eyes, that meant you and her.

Mike1991: Well, I did look up, I remember.

Sally1974: When you're on this outing with her and her friends, then you should emphasize the group less than her directly. Use your eyes and your hands with your words.

Alex1986: Mike, if you don't usually use your hands when you talk, don't overdo it. I had a friend that moved his hands when he talked, and how much he moves his hands shows how excited he is or how nervous he is. If you just want to be friends with this girl and her friends, then you don't want to look over-jealous with her in any way. If you can look over-interested in any group activity, that may get her to back off. Of course she may think she could use this activity to get closer with you.

John2010: I showed you how to let someone know that they are acting inappropriately with witty comebacks that may help with this girl, to show less care for her.

Mike1991: I don't want to hurt her!

Anna1983: Yes, some of the things John has taught us do seem mean, but in this situation it may be better to rip the Band-Aid off quickly.

Amy1979: Some of the things John is suggesting are just smart. I mean, that note thing he encouraged me to do on Wednesday was genius. I left a note by the toilet Jim always uses, and before sitting down at the couch, Jim had a smile and said to me, "I rinsed my hands. Did I do a good job?"

Jill1959: Those notes do help with encouragements. Anna is right, I don't feel right taking advantage of my friends, but at work it's just to get ahead. I have used emotional communication with my family, because I was concerned, and with my new friends just to know them better.

Sledge1984: Yeah, I got to know my extended family much better these past weeks. I have seen how my sister has changed by building her jar of life. I've come to the conclusion that she has an unwarranted crush on my brother-in-law. Things are happening in her life that make her uncomfortable, and she thinks he's safe.

Sally1974: From what I've read about your brother-in-law, he doesn't seem that stable.

Sledge1984: Oh, he's not, but she doesn't see that. I have gotten more involved with her life and started to tell her about Andy, what I've learned about him these past weeks, but I use emotional communication; I don't point out the negative points right away. I have pointed out some things as being good that I know she'd think as bad…

Tarry1978: Oh, I did that too. With Jamie I was talking about her new friends pointing out things that she wouldn't like, but I was too influential. She gave me a questionable look and I clammed up. I was afraid she would think I actually liked it. A minute later I started to explain, but luckily she moved on. I was thinking, I shouldn't try to explain a lie.

John2010: That's right, when you see things aren't going your way, I would move on to something you both enjoy and let it pass. If you try to explain yourself, then it will stick, and it may make it harder next time.

Rick1982: Sorry I'm late for John's farewell party.

Sally1974: What? John's not going anywhere…

John2010: Thanks, Rick! Read the posts. Yes, today will be my last scheduled night with you.

Bill4267: I was wondering why there were so many people here chatting about how you have helped them.

John2010: I just don't have anything else to help you with.

Sally1974: What? That relationship with that guy from work. I think I like him.

Mike1991: Yeah, what if I end up liking this other girl?

Sledge1984: How am I going to set up my sister with Andy and then stop it?

Alex1986: I have been reading today's posts and it looks like you all could help me.

John2010: That's right! Thank you, Alex. Just because I won't be here doesn't mean you all can't help each other.

Rick1982: Well, I am getting along much better with Crista. I just needed to listen to her better and I wouldn't have known to do that if it wasn't for you, John. You all did give me good advice.

Timmy1982: Yeah, we just need someone to organize it.

Anna1983: Yeah, how will we know who to listen to?

John2010: Listen to them all. Alex has shared a number of experiences that he has had. Now, that is a good way to give advice and remember lessens. Your weekly journals should have a number of these stories to share. If they don't and you're just a fact checker, then make a section just for these stories, and you can be as vague as you want.

Amy1979: You want us to share our life stories with each other. Well, I have some personal stuff that I've written in my diary.

John2010: I did say that you can be vague. Write it as if you are talking about someone else and the facts can be fiction.

Timmy1982: John, that story you added to our e-mails last week told us that sharing bad experience's isn't good.

John2010: Well, I thought that paper was self-explanatory, but the message I was trying to convey was not to overdo it. When you are relating to someone's experience, don't say to them or to yourself, "I know how you feel." One thing is that you can't, and do you really want to?

Sally1974: Well, I would want to know how my friends feel.

John2010: You don't want to feel the pain and heartache. A good way to relieve yourself from the situation is to put it in the context of just being a story. Let's not talk about how TV is desensitizing our children.

There was a lot of chatter before John2010 logged off, but they nearly named Alex as the leader of the club. John did write a final letter to them all with specific details for each of them and wishing them luck in all their ventures.

Note from the Author

J. L. Manning thought that this book would help the common person see how the little things matter. He wrote these twelve unfinished stories hoping that the readers could finish one if not all of the stories with encounters from their own lives.

These stories are all fiction, as fiction as it gets, from the life of any fiction author. Don't think any of these characters represent J. L. Manning. If anything, all of his many characters do. If you get anything from this book, don't overlook that you shouldn't share too much on-line.